ESSENTIAL FRENCH

Nicole Irving & Leslie Colvin
Illustrated by Ann Johns
Designed by Adrienne Kern
Additional designs by Brian Robertson

Language consultants: Renée Chaspoul
& Annick Dunbar
Series editor: Gaby Waters

Contents

About this book

This phrase book will help you to survive, travel and socialize. It supplies simple, up-to-date French for holidays and exchange visits. It also gives basic information about France and tips for low budget travellers.

The language is everyday, spoken French. This can differ from textbook French and ranges from the correct to the colloquial, and from the polite to the casual, depending on the region, the situation and the person speaking.

Use the Contents list to find the section you need or look up words in the Index. Always remember that you can make yourself clear with words that are not quite right or with very few words. Saying "Paris?" while pointing at a train will provoke oui or non (yes or no). Words like pardon (excuse me) or merci (thank you) make anything sound more polite and generally guarantee a friendly response. For anyone who is ready to have a go, the French listed below is absolutely essential.

●Newcomers to French should look through French pronunciation and How French works (pages 50-53).

●Words are given in the form likely to be most useful. The level of politeness is pitched to suit each situation and casual tu or polite vous forms are given as appropriate. Sometimes you will have to judge which is best so both are given. If in doubt, say vous.

●An asterisk after a French word shows it is slang or fairly familiar, e.g. boring rasoir*.

●(m) is short for masculine, and (f) for feminine.

●Adjectives with two forms are given twice: masculine/feminine, e.g. green vert/verte.

Absolute essentials

Do you speak English?	Vous parlez anglais?[1]	1 un	11 onze
	Tu parles anglais?[2]	2 deux	12 douze
I don't understand.	Je ne comprends pas.	3 trois	13 treize
Can you write it down?	Vous pouvez me l'écrire?[1]	4 quatre	14 quatorze
	Tu peux me l'écrire?[2]	5 cinq	15 quinze
Can you say that again?	Vous pouvez répéter ça?[1]	6 six	16 seize
	Tu peux répéter ça?[2]	7 sept	17 dix-sept
A bit slower, please.	Un peu plus lentement, s'il vous plaît.	8 huit	18 dix-huit
What does this word mean?	Que veut dire ce mot?	9 neuf	19 dix-neuf
What's the French for this?	Comment on dit ça en français?	10 dix	20 vingt

yes	oui	hi	salut	why?	pourquoi?
no	non	bye	salut	because	parce que
maybe	peut-être	good morning	bonjour	how?	comment?
I don't know.	Je ne sais pas.	good evening	bonsoir	how much?	combien?
I don't mind.	Ça m'est égal.	good night	bonne nuit	How much is it?	C'est combien?
please	s'il vous plaît[1]	see you soon	à bientôt	how many?	combien?
	s'il te plaît[2]	Mr, Sir	Monsieur[3]	What is it/this?	Qu'est-ce que c'est?
thank you	merci	Mrs, Madam	Madame[3]		C'est quoi?
sorry	désolé/désolée	Miss	Mademoiselle[3]	it/this is	c'est
excuse me	pardon	and	et	is there?	est-ce qu'il y a?
I'm very sorry	je suis désolé/désolée	or	ou	there is	il y a?
hello	bonjour	when?	quand?	I'd like	je voudrais
goodbye	au revoir	where?	où?	could I have?	je peux avoir?

[1]Polite form. See page 52. [2]Familiar form. See page 52. [3]In French these are often used on their own, without a name. See page 12.

Je suis perdu.
I'm lost.

Vous pouvez m'aider,
s'il vous plaît?
Can you help me, please?

Où est le Syndicat
d'initiative?
Where is the tourist
office?

Vous pouvez me dessiner
un plan?
Can you draw me a map?

Est-ce qu'il y a des
toilettes publiques par ici?
Is there a public toilet
around here?

Fact file

Most big towns and cities have a *Syndicat d'initiative* (tourist office), sometimes called *Office du tourisme* – abbreviated to *SI* or *OT*. It's often near the station or town hall. In tourist areas even small towns have one but opening times may be restricted or erratic.

Most tourist offices will provide town plans and leaflets on local sights free of charge. They also give advice on places to stay and travel arrangements. They often employ someone who speaks English. Some tourist offices sell maps and specialist booklets on local footpaths, wildlife etc., although these may be in French.

Directions

It's on the left/right.	*C'est à gauche/droite.*
Go left/right.	*Allez à gauche/droite.*
Go straight ahead.	*Allez tout droit.*
Take the first on the left.	*Prenez la première rue à gauche.*
Take the second turning on the right.	*Prenez le deuxième tournant à droite.*
Follow the signs for Blois.	*Suivez les panneaux pour Blois.*
It's...	*C'est...*
Go...	*Allez...*
Carry on...	*Continuez...*
straight ahead	*tout droit*
Turn...	*Tournez...*
left	*à gauche*
right	*à droite*
Take...	*Prenez...*
the first	*le premier/la première*
the second	*le/la deuxième*
the third	*le/la troisième*
the fourth	*le/la quatrième*
turning	*le tournant*
on the left	*à gauche*
on the right	*à droite*
crossroads, junction	*le carrefour*
roundabout	*le rond-point*
traffic lights	*les feux*
pedestrian crossing	*le passage clouté*
subway	*le passage souterrain*
Cross...	*Traversez...*
Follow...	*Suivez...*
street	*la rue, le boulevard[1]*
road	*la route*
alley	*la ruelle*
path	*le chemin, le sentier*
main street	*la rue principale*
high street	*la grand-rue*
square	*la place, le square*

[1] *Un boulevard* is usually a broad, leafy street in a city.

motorway	l'autoroute
ringroad	le boulevard périphérique
one way	sens unique
no entry	sens interdit
dead end	cul-de-sac
no parking	stationnement interdit
car park	un parking
parking meters	des parcmètres
pedestrian area	une zone piétonnière
pedestrians	piétons
pavement	le trottoir
town centre	le centre de la ville
in town, to town	en ville
area, part of town	le quartier
outskirts, suburbs	la banlieue
town hall	la mairie, l'hôtel de ville
bridge	le pont
river	la rivière
railway line	la ligne de chemin de fer
post office	la poste, les PTT
shops	les magasins
church	l'église
school	l'école
cinema	le cinéma
museum	le musée
park	le jardin public
just before the	juste avant le/la
just after the	juste après le/la
to the end of	jusqu'au bout de
on the corner	au coin
next to	près de
opposite	en face de
in front of	devant
behind	derrière
above	au-dessus, en haut
beneath	au-dessous, en bas
over	par-dessus
under	en dessous
in	dans
on	sur
here	ici
there	là
over there	là-bas
far	loin
close, near	près (de)
nearby	tout près, juste à côté
near here	près d'ici
around here	dans les alentours, par ici
somewhere	quelque part
in this area	dans ce quartier
10 minutes walk	à dix minutes de marche
5 minutes drive	à cinq minutes en voiture
by bike	en vélo
on foot	à pied

5

Travel: trains, underground, buses

Getting information

What time is the next train to Toulouse?

How long is the journey?

Do I have to change?

Tickets

Where can I buy a ticket?

How does this machine work?

Can I have a single to Avignon?

Finding the right bus

Is this the right bus for Versailles?

Where does this bus go?

Can you tell me where to get off?

Je change où pour la gare St-Lazare?

C'est quel quai pour Les Halles?

Qu'est-ce qu'on vient d'annoncer?

| Where do I change for St-Lazare? | What did they just say over the loudspeaker? | Which platform for Les Halles? |

J'ai droit à une réduction?

Can I get a reduction?

Fact file

The *SNCF* (French railways) runs an extensive rail network and operates some bus services. Fares are cheaper on off-peak *jours bleus* (blue days). Before you get on a train, look for the sign *Compostez votre billet* (Stamp your ticket), stamp it in the machine then hang on to it. *TGV* are high speed trains – you reserve in advance and pay a supplement. There are various cheap deals, e.g. *France Vacances* for two or four weeks travel or *Carte Jeune* (youth railcard) for half price fares in the summer.

The Paris *métro* is easy to use if you have a map – free from stations. Check the number of the line you want and the direction – the last stop on the line gives you this, e.g. *Direction Pont de Neuilly*. The same tickets are valid on the *métro*, buses[1] and the central zone of the *RER* (Paris express trains). A book of ten tickets or a *Carte Orange* (travel pass) usually work out cheaper than single tickets. Books of tickets are available from *tabacs* (tobacconists, see page 23) as well as stations.

railway station	la gare	ticket (train)	un billet
underground station	la station de métro	a single	un aller simple
bus station	la gare routière	a return	un aller et retour
bus stop	l'arrêt d'autobus	book of tickets	un carnet de tickets
train	le train	supplement	un supplément
underground train	le métro	I'd like to reserve a	Je voudrais réserver
tram	le tramway	seat.	une place.
bus	l'autobus	left luggage locker	le casier de consigne
coach	le car	track [3]	la voie
leaves at 2 [2]	part à deux heures	connection	une correspondance
arrives at 4	arrive à quatre heures	timetable	l'horaire
first/last	le premier/le dernier	arrivals/departures	arrivées/départs
next	le prochain	long distance	grandes lignes
cheapest	le moins cher	local, suburban	banlieue
ticket office	le guichet	every day	tous les jours
ticket machine	un distributeur automatique	weekdays [2]	semaine
fare	le tarif	Sundays and holidays	dimanches et fêtes
student fare	tarif étudiant	in the summer time	pendant l'été
youth fare	tarif jeune	out of season	hors saison
ticket (bus and tube)	un ticket	except	sauf

[1]Long bus journeys in Paris and some other cities may cost you two tickets. [2]For times, days of the week etc. see page 54. [3]Each *quai* (platform) has two *voies* (tracks or sides).

Travel: air, sea, road

Air and sea

Je voudrais confirmer mon vol.

I'd like to confirm my flight.

A quelle heure je dois faire enregistrer les bagages?

What time should I check in?

Où est-ce que je fais enregistrer mes bagages?

Where do I check in?

Mes bagages ne sont pas arrivés.

My luggage hasn't arrived.

Madame Duclos est supposée me rencontrer.

Mrs Duclos is supposed to be meeting me.

Fact file

Airports and harbours usually have signs and announcements in English. There's often a *navette* (bus shuttle) from the airport into town.

Taxis have a standard pick-up charge plus a metered fare; each large bag is charged extra. Taxis often take only three passengers, but can still be good value.

Emmenez-moi au/à la¹...
Take me to...
C'est combien pour aller au/à la¹...?
What's the fare to...?
Laissez-moi ici, s'il vous plaît.
Please drop me here.

airport	*l'aéroport*	customs	*douane*
port	*le port*	visa	*le visa*
aeroplane	*l'avion*	passport	*le passeport*
ferry	*le ferry*	departure gate	*la porte (de départ)*
hovercraft	*l'aéroglisseur*	boarding pass	*la carte*
flight	*le vol*		*d'embarquement*
(sea) crossing	*la traversée*	foot passenger	*passager sans véhicule*
the English Channel	*la Manche*	No smoking section	*Non-fumeurs*
rough	*agité/agitée*		
calm	*calme*	travel agent	*l'agence de voyages*
I feel sea sick.	*J'ai le mal de mer.*	airline ticket	*un billet d'avion*
on board	*à bord*	cut price	*à prix réduit*
suitcase	*une valise*	standby	*sans garantie*
backpack, rucksack	*un sac à dos*	charter flight	*un vol charter*
bag	*un sac*	flight number	*le numéro de vol*
hand luggage	*des bagages à main*	a booking	*une réservation*
heavy	*lourd/lourde*	to change	*changer*
trolley	*un chariot*	to cancel	*annuler*
information	*renseignements*	a delay	*un retard*

¹Use *au* + (m), *à la* + (f) place names. See page 51. ²Literally, "traffic coming from the right has right of way". ³There is a toll on French motorways. ⁴See page 41 for kinds of bikes. ⁵It's not

On the road

> Je suis tombé en panne.

> Où est le garage le plus proche?

I've broken down.   Where's the nearest garage?

> Je ne sais pas ce qui ne va pas.

> Vous pouvez réparer ça?

> Les freins ne marchent pas.

I don't know what's wrong.   Can you fix it?   The brakes don't work.

Fact file

You can hire bikes from train stations or bike shops. On shorter train journeys, you can travel with a bike at no extra cost – see *SNCF* leaflet *Guide du train et du vélo*. You can ride mopeds from age 14, but must be insured and wear a helmet. Remember the French drive on the right. When you get to a town, follow signs for *Toutes/Autres directions* (all/other directions) until you see the signs you want.

town centre	centre-ville	car	une voiture, une bagnole*
give way	cédez le passage, priorité à droite [2]	bicycle [4]	une bicyclette
toll	péage [3]	bike	un vélo
insurance	l'assurance	moped	un vélomoteur
driving licence	le permis de conduire	motorbike	une moto
(car) documents	les papiers	battery	la batterie
crash helmet	un casque	radiator	le radiateur
petrol station	une station-service	to hitch [5]	faire du stop
petrol	de l'essence	lights	les phares
lead-free petrol	de l'essence sans plomb	chain	la chaîne
oil/petrol mixture	du mélange	wheel	la roue
		gears	les vitesses
oil	de l'huile	cable	le câble
litre	un litre	brakes	les freins
		pump	la pompe
		tyre	le pneu
		inner tube	la chambre à air

garage, repair shop	un garage
I have a puncture.	J'ai crevé.
Fill it up, please.	Le plein, s'il vous plaît.
The engine won't start.	Le moteur ne démarre pas.
The battery's flat.	La batterie est à plat.
How much will it cost?	Ça va coûter combien?
Can I hire...?	Je voudrais louer...
for hire	à louer

Travel talk

> Tu vas où? [6].
> Where are you going?

> Je vais à St-Jean-de-Luz.
> I'm going to St Jean de Luz.

> Tu es allé à Biarritz? [7]
> Have you been to Biarritz?

> C'est comment?
> What's it like?

advisable to hitch, but there are ride sharing organizations such as *Allôstop*. [6]/[7]The polite forms are: [6]*Vous allez où?* [7]*Vous êtes allé à Biarritz?* **See page 52.**

Accommodation: places to stay

At the Tourist office

Vous avez une liste de campings?

Je cherche une chambre pour deux personnes.

Vous pouvez me réserver une chambre?

Do you have a list of campsites?

I'm looking for a room for two people.

Can you book a room for me?

Hotels

Vous avez une chambre?

C'est complet.

Vous connaissez un autre hôtel par ici?

Do you have a room?

We're full.

Is there another hotel nearby?

Fact file

The *Syndicat d'initiative* or *Office du tourisme* (tourist office) will supply lists of places to stay.

Cheap accommodation includes 1 and 2 star *hôtels*. Most have rooms for three/four people which cuts costs. *Demi-pension* (half-board) and *pension* (full board) can be good value.

Other cheap options are: *auberges de jeunesse* (youth hostels)[1] – a good idea in towns and cities; *gîtes d'étape* – basic hostels in walking or cycling areas; *relais routiers* – restaurants with basic rooms; *chambres d'hôte* – bed and breakfast.

There are lots of *campings* (campsites). The local *camping municipal* is often the cheapest.

Camping

Il y a un emplacement de libre?

Do you have a space?

[1]You need to be a member of the IYHA (International Youth Hostel Association). You may be able to join on the spot.

Rooms to let	Chambres à louer, Chambres d'hôte
How much do you want to pay?	Combien vous voulez payer?
How many nights?	Combien de nuits?
One/two night(s).	Une/deux nuit(s).
room	une chambre
single...	...pour une personne
double...	...pour deux personnes
...with 3 beds	...avec trois lits
clean	propre
cheap	pas cher/chère
expensive	cher/chère
lunch	le déjeuner
dinner (evening)	le dîner
key	la clé
room number	le numéro de la chambre
registration form	une fiche

Can I have my passport back?	Vous pouvez me rendre mon passeport?
tent	une tente
caravan	une caravane
restaurant	un restaurant
swimming pool	une piscine
hot water	l'eau chaude
cold water	l'eau froide
drinking water	l'eau potable
camping gas	une cartouche de camping-gaz
guy rope, rope	une corde
tent rings	des caoutchoucs de bas de tente
tent peg	un piquet
mallet	un maillet
torch	une lampe de poche
matches	des allumettes
loo paper	du papier hygiénique
can opener	un ouvre-boîte

Combien coûte la chambre?

How much for a room?

Le petit déjeuner est compris?

Does that include breakfast?

Je peux voir la chambre?

Can I see the room?

On est trois avec une tente.

There are three of us with a tent.

Il y a un magasin?

Do you have a shop?

On peut boire l'eau du robinet?

Is it OK to drink the tap water?

Où est-ce qu'on peut aller se baigner?

Where's the best place to swim?

Accommodation: staying with people

Greetings

Bonjour.
Hello.

Comment ça va?
How are you?

For more polite or formal greetings, say *Bonjour* (hello) followed by *Monsieur* or *Madame* (see page 3). Also use the polite *vous* form: *Comment allez-vous?* (How are you?)

Où est-ce que je peux mettre mes affaires?

Je dors où?

Where can I put my things?

Where am I sleeping?

A quelle heure est le petit déjeuner?

Tu peux me réveiller à sept heures?[1]

What time do you have breakfast?

Could you wake me up at seven?

Washing

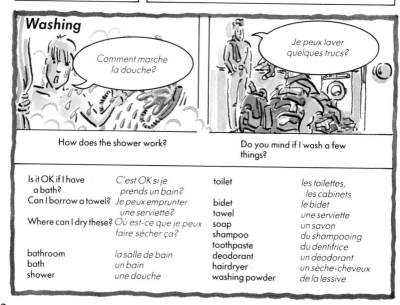

Comment marche la douche?

Je peux laver quelques trucs?

How does the shower work?

Do you mind if I wash a few things?

Is it OK if I have a bath?	C'est OK si je prends un bain?	toilet	les toilettes, les cabinets
Can I borrow a towel?	Je peux emprunter une serviette?	bidet	le bidet
Where can I dry these?	Où est-ce que je peux faire sécher ça?	towel	une serviette
		soap	un savon
		shampoo	du shampooing
		toothpaste	du dentifrice
bathroom	la salle de bain	deodorant	un déodorant
bath	un bain	hairdryer	un sèche-cheveux
shower	une douche	washing powder	de la lessive

[1]To be polite, when speaking to a stranger or an older person, use *vous: Vous pouvez me réveiller* etc. See page 52.

Being polite

Je peux payer quelque chose?

Non, ne t'inquiète pas.

Can I pay my share?   No, don't worry.

C'est gentil à vous de me recevoir.

Je demanderai si j'ai besoin de quelque chose.

It's nice of you to let me stay.   I'll ask if I need anything.

Saying goodbye

Merci pour tout.
Thank you for everything.

Au revoir.
Goodbye.

Using the phone

Je peux utiliser votre téléphone?
Can I use your phone?

Je veux payer la communication.
I'll pay for the call.

C'est combien pour appeler l'Angleterre?
How much is it to call Britain?

See page 15 for more about phones and making phone calls.

I'm tired.	Je suis fatigué/fatiguée.
I'm knackered.	Je suis crevé/crevée.
I'm cold/hot.	J'ai froid/chaud.
Everything's OK.	Tout va bien.
Can I have a key?	Je peux avoir une clé?
What is there to do in the evenings?	Qu'est-ce qu'on peut faire le soir?
Where's the nearest phone box?	Où est la cabine téléphonique la plus proche?
alarm clock	un réveil
sleeping bag	un sac de couchage
on the floor	par terre
an extra...	un/une autre...
blanket	une couverture
quilt, duvet	une couette
sheet	un drap
pillow	un oreiller
bolster[2]	un traversin, un polochon
electric socket	une prise
needle	une aiguille
thread	du fil
scissors	des ciseaux
iron	un fer à repasser
upstairs	en haut
downstairs	en bas
cupboard	un placard
bedroom	la chambre
living room	le salon
kitchen	la cuisine
garden	le jardin
balcony	le balcon

[2]A long, tube shaped pillow often used in France.

Banks, post offices, phones

Banks

Je voudrais changer de l'argent.

I want to change this.

Vous prenez les eurochèques?

Je peux voir votre passeport?

Do you accept Eurocheques?   Can I see your passport?

Money problems

J'ai perdu mes traveller's chèques.

I've lost my traveller's cheques.

Les numéros de la série sont ...

Comment je fais pour en avoir d'autres?

The serial numbers were...   How do I get replacements?

Phones[1]

Ce téléphone ne marche pas.

This phone doesn't work.

C'est bien l'indicatif pour Lyon?

Is this the code for Lyons?

Allô, Sylvie est là s'il vous plaît?

Hello, is Sylvie there please?

[1]For more phrases on using the phone see page 13.

bank	une banque	letter	une lettre
cashier's desk, till	la caisse	parcel	un colis
foreign exchange	bureau de change	a stamp for	un timbre pour
enquiries	bureau de renseignements	Britain	l'Angleterre
		the USA	les États-Unis
money	de l'argent	Australia[2]	l'Australie
small change	de la monnaie	by airmail	par avion
notes	des billets	by registered post	en recommandé
traveller's cheques	des traveller's chèques, des chèques de voyage	poste restante	poste restante
eurocheques	des eurochèques	telephone	un téléphone
credit card	une carte de crédit	telephone box	une cabine téléphonique
exchange rate	le cours du change	directory	un annuaire
commission	la commission	phone number	le numéro de téléphone
money transfer from London	une mise à disposition de Londres	wrong number	le mauvais numéro
post office	une poste, les PTT	reverse charge call	un appel en PCV
postcard	une carte postale	Hang on.	Ne quittez pas.

Post offices

J'attends de l'argent, il est arrivé?

I'm expecting some money, has it arrived?

Je voudrais un timbre pour envoyer ça.

Can I have a stamp for this?

Pardon, il y a une boîte aux lettres par ici?

Where's the nearest postbox?

Elle rentre quand?
When will she be back?

Je peux laisser un message pour...?
Can I leave a message for...?

Dites-lui que j'ai appelé, s'il vous plaît.
Please tell her/him I called.

Elle/il peut me rappeler?
Can she/he call me back?

Mon numéro est le...
My number is...

Fact file

The unit of currency is the French *franc* (FF). 1 FF = 100 *centimes*. Banking hours vary. Most banks are open Monday to Friday 9-12 and 2-4. Some open on Saturday and close on Monday. *Bureaux de change* (foreign exchange offices) are often open outside banking hours but may give a poorer exchange rate.

Phone boxes take coins but many take *télécartes* (phonecards). The blue bell symbol means you can receive incoming calls. There are also public phones in post offices and cafés. These are often metered and you pay after the call.

You can buy phonecards and stamps from post offices or *tabacs* (see page 22). For useful phone numbers see page 47.

[2]For other countries see page 55.

Cafés

café	un café, un bar, un café-brasserie
chair	une chaise
table	une table
at the bar	au comptoir
Cheers!	A ta/votre santé![1]
something to drink	quelque chose à boire
something to eat	quelque chose à manger
snack	un casse-croûte
black coffee	un café, un express
(large) white coffee	un (grand) crème
small	petit
tea	un thé
tea with milk	un thé au lait
hot chocolate	un chocolat chaud
fruit juice	un jus de fruit
orange juice	un jus d'orange
coke	un coca
mineral water	de l'eau minérale
still	plate
fizzy	gazeuse
beer (bottled)	une bière
(draught)	une pression, un demi
glass of red wine	un verre de vin rouge
bottle of ...	une bouteille de ...
half a bottle of white wine	une demi-bouteille de vin blanc
milk	du lait
sugar	du sucre
with ice	avec des glaçons
slice of lemon	une tranche de citron
cheese/ham sandwich	un sandwich au fromage/jambon
omelette	une omelette
ice-cream	une glace

Fact file

Cafés are open 7 am to 10 pm or later for drinks, snacks, meeting up with friends or using the loo and phone. Prices vary (smart means pricey). If you sit down a waiter serves you. Drinks are cheaper if you stand at the bar.
Cafés serve breakfast (see pages 21 and 25). Snacks include *croque-monsieur* (toasted ham and cheese sandwich), omelettes (*nature* is a plain one) and sandwiches, usually a piece of *baguette* (French bread) with cheese or meat.
Tea comes with lemon — ask for milk if you want it. Bottled beers are pricey, draught beer is cheaper. Try *citron pressé* (freshly squeezed lemon) — you add your own water and sugar.

On prend un café?
How about a cup of coffee?

Cette chaise est libre?
Is this chair free?

Je peux voir la carte?
Can I see the menu?

Un café, s'il vous plaît.
A black coffee, please.

Vous avez des milk-shakes?
Do you have milkshakes?

[1]Say *A ta santé* to a friend. *A votre santé* is the polite singular or the plural form. See page 52.

17

Eating out[1]

Choosing a place

On va où?

Je n'aime pas les pizzas.

Si on allait manger un hamburger?

Where shall we go? I don't like pizzas. What about a hamburger?

French food	la cuisine française	chips	des frites
Moroccan food	la cuisine marocaine	sausages	des saucisses
cheap restaurant	un restaurant pas cher	mixed salad	une salade composée
fast-food restaurant (hamburgers etc.)	un fast-food	green salad	une salade verte
take-away	à emporter	spaghetti	des spaghettis
menu	la carte	rare	saignant
starter	l'entrée	medium	à point
main course	le plat principal	well done	bien cuit
dessert	le dessert		
price	le prix	mustard	la moutarde
soup	de la soupe, du potage	salt	le sel
fish	du poisson	pepper	le poivre
meat	de la viande	dressing	la vinaigrette
vegetables	des légumes	mayonnaise	la mayonnaise
cheese	du fromage		
fruit	des fruits	Is everything all right?	Tout va bien?
		Yes, it's very good.	Oui, c'est très bon.

Problems

Ce n'est pas assez cuit.

J'ai demandé un steak frites.

Vous n'avez pas de ketchup?

I ordered steak and chips. This isn't cooked enough. Don't you have any ketchup?

[1]There are also food words on pages 16, 21 and 25.

Deciding what to have

C'est quoi, ça?

J'en veux un comme ça.

Je peux en avoir un sans fromage?

What's that?	I'll have one of those.	Can I have one without cheese?

Fact file

Standard French dishes are *steak frites* or *poulet frites* (steak or chicken and chips). Try the *specialités régionales* (regional specialities) or *couscous* (a North African dish). Red meat is often served rare. Ask for *très, très cuit* to get it very well done.

There are lots of *restaurants*, sometimes called *brasserie*. Many are quite cheap. Look out for *le menu, menu du jour* or *menu touristique* (set menu) which is displayed outside with its price. It is usually three courses and can be cheap. *Le plat du jour* (dish of the day) is often good value. Cheap places to eat are *pizzerias* (pizza places), *crêperies* for *crêpes*

(pancakes with various fillings) and fast-food places. These are easy to recognize.

Cafés do snacks and simple meals (see page 16) but they can be pricey.

Tipping in cafés and restaurants is normal practice but *Service compris* means service is included. *Service non compris* means it is not so it's best to leave a tip of about 10%.

Best times for eating out are lunch at 12 or 1 and dinner at about 8.

It's often cheaper to buy your own food (see page 25).

S'il vous plaît!

Excuse me!

L'addition s'il vous plaît.

Can we have the bill please?

Je n'ai pas demandé ça.

I didn't order this.

Eating in

Helping

| Can I help? | Can I lay the table? | Can I do the washing-up? |

[1] The polite forms are *Vous pouvez me passer . . ., Vous voulez . . .* and *Je peux vous aider?*
See page 52.

Ça me suffit, merci.
I've had enough thanks.

C'était délicieux.
That was delicious.

meal	*le repas*	pasta	*des pâtes*
breakfast	*le petit déjeuner*	rice	*du riz*
lunch	*le déjeuner*	dried beans	*des haricots secs*
dinner (evening)	*le dîner*	potatoes	*des pommes de terre*
		onions	*des oignons*
bowl	*un bol*	garlic	*de l'ail*
glass	*un verre*	tomatoes	*des tomates*
plate	*une assiette*	peppers	*des poivrons*
knife	*un couteau*	green beans	*des haricots verts*
fork	*une fourchette*		
spoon	*une cuillère*	peas	*des petits pois*
		courgettes	*des courgettes*
cereal	*des céréales*	aubergines	*des aubergines*
bread	*du pain*		
jam	*de la confiture*	spinach	*des épinards*
margarine	*de la margarine*	cabbage	*du chou*
		cauliflower	*du chou-fleur*
		chicory	*des endives*
chicken	*du poulet*	raw	*cru/crue*
pork	*du porc*	(too) hot, spicy	*(trop) relevé/relevée*
beef	*du boeuf*		
veal	*du veau*	salty	*salé/salée*
liver	*du foie*	sweet	*sucré/sucrée*

Enjoy your meal.	*Bon appétit!*
I'm hungry/thirsty.	*J'ai faim/soif.*
I'm not hungry.	*Je n'ai pas faim.*

Fact file

Breakfast is coffee (or tea or hot chocolate) with a *croissant* or *tartine* (bread with butter and jam). At home *café au lait* (coffee and plenty of hot milk) served in a bowl is standard and it's fine to dunk whatever you are eating.

Meals are often three courses. Salad can be a separate course. Cheese comes before pudding which is often fruit.

Special cases

Je n'aime pas le poisson.

I don't like fish.

Je suis végétarien[2].

I'm a vegetarian.

Je ne supporte pas les oeufs.

I'm allergic to eggs.

[2]If you're a girl, say *végétarienne*.

Shopping

Can I help you?   I'd like that.

How much is it?

86 francs.

Please write that down.

That's fine.   I'll take it.

Shops

shopping centre	un centre commercial
shop	un magasin
department store	un grand magasin
market	le marché
hypermarket	un hypermarché
supermarket	un supermarché, un libre-service
small supermarket	alimentation générale
grocer	une épicerie
baker	une boulangerie
cake shop	une pâtisserie
sweet shop	une confiserie
butcher	une boucherie
delicatessen	une charcuterie, un traiteur
fruit/veg stall, greengrocer	un marchand de fruits et légumes
fishmonger	une poissonnerie
health food shop	un magasin de produits diététiques
hardware shop	une droguerie, une quincaillerie
chemist	une pharmacie
camera shop	un magasin de photo
gift shop	cadeaux
tobacconist	un tabac, un bar-tabac
newsagent	un marchand de journaux
bookshop	une librairie
stationer	une papeterie
record shop	un magasin de disques, un disquaire
flea market	marché aux puces
sports shop	un magasin de sport
heel bar	talon minute
hairdresser, barber	un coiffeur
launderette	une laverie automatique
travel agent	une agence de tourisme
browsers welcome[1]	entrée libre[1]
open	ouvert/ouverte
closed	fermé/fermée
entrance	l'entrée
exit	la sortie
check-out	la caisse
stairs	l'escalier
price	le prix

[1] *Entrée libre* is a sign you often see in shop windows. Its literal translation is "free entry", and simply means you should feel free to look around.

Fact file

Opening times vary but bear in mind that many shops close for lunch and close on Monday. Most shops are open Tuesday to Saturday 9 to 12 and 2 to 7. Small food shops may open on Sunday morning and others on Monday. Department stores and big supermarkets stay open all day Monday to Saturday. In the south, shops open earlier, close longer for lunch and stay open later. Look out for signs on shop doors: *Heures d'ouverture* (opening hours) or *Fermeture hebdomadaire* (closed each week on...).[2] A *tabac*, sometimes part of a bar, sells stamps, phonecards, sweets, cigarettes etc., and may sell bus/*métro* tickets. *Drogueries* sell handy things for camping but try a *magasin de sport* for camping equipment. *Pharmacies* sell make-up, soap, etc., as well as medicines but everyday things are cheaper in chain stores such as *Monoprix* or *Prisunic* or in supermarkets.

The cheapest and easiest way to buy food is in a hypermarket or supermarket. Specialist shops may be more pricey, but offer more choice and are worth a visit. *Charcuteries* or *traiteurs* sell salads, quiches, pizzas, etc., as well as *charcuterie* (cured and cold meats, pâté, salami...). In small places with no baker, the sign *dépôt de pain* means fresh bread is stocked. Markets are held regularly. They're colourful and lively as well as being good for food, local produce, cheap clothes etc. There are few greengrocers. People buy fruit and vegetables from market stalls or supermarkets and *alimentation générale* stores.

Finding the right place

Où sont les magasins?

Vous vendez des piles?

Où est-ce que je peux en trouver?

Where's the main shopping area?

Do you sell batteries?

Where can I get some?

Où est-ce que je peux faire réparer ça?

Where can I get this repaired?

Où est-ce que je peux trouver des lunettes de soleil?

Where's a good place for sunglasses?

[2]See page 54 for days, dates and times.

I need some sun-tan lotion.

Is there a bigger one?

sunscreen[1]	un écran total	plasters	du sparadrap	sunglasses	des lunettes de soleil
make-up	du maquillage				
(hair) gel	du gel (pour les cheveux)	film	une pellicule	jewellery	des bijoux
		English newspapers	des journaux anglais	watch	une montre
hair spray	de la laque			earrings	des boucles d'oreilles
tampons	des tampons	postcard	une carte postale		
tissues	des mouchoirs en papier	writing paper	du papier à lettres	ring	une bague
		envelope	une enveloppe	purse	un porte-monnaie
razor	un rasoir	notebook	un carnet		
shaving foam	de la crème à raser	pen	un stylo	bag	un sac
aspirin	de l'aspirine	pencil	un crayon	smaller	plus petit/petite
contact lens solution	de la solution de nettoyage (pour lentilles)	poster	une affiche	cheaper	moins cher/chère
		stickers	des autocollants	another colour	d'une autre couleur
		badges	des badges		

Can I help you?   I'm just looking.

Can I see that?

How much is it?

I'll think about it.

[1]See page 12 for other everyday things. [2]You can buy half: *une demi-baguette*, or *une ficelle* (a thin baguette).

I'd like a French stick. [2]

Can I have 15 francs worth of grapes?

Can I have a bit of that pâté?

Like that?

A bit more please.

Ok, that's enough thanks.

carrier-bag	un sac plastique	croissant	un croissant
small	petit/petite		une brioche[3]
big	gros/grosse		un pain au chocolat[3]
a slice of	une tranche de		un pain aux raisins[3]
a bit more	un peu plus	doughnut	un beignet
a bit less	un peu moins	sweets	des bonbons
a portion of	une part de	chocolate	du chocolat
a piece of	un morceau de	crisps	des chips
a kilogram	un kilo	peanuts	des cacahuètes
half a kilo	une livre	fruit	des fruits
250 grammes	deux cent cinquante grammes	apples	des pommes
		pears	des poires
health food	produits diététiques	peaches	des pêches
organic	biologique, naturel	nectarines	des brugnons
		plums	des prunes
French salami	du saucisson	apricots	des abricots
quiche	une quiche (lorraine)	figs	des figues
bread	du pain	cherries	des cerises
wholemeal bread	du pain complet	strawberries	des fraises
roll	un petit pain	raspberries	des framboises
cake	un gâteau	melon	un melon

[3]There's no useful translation for these. Try them as alternatives to a croissant.

[4]See pages 16-21 for more food words.

Clothes

Can I try this on?   Do you have it in a small?   I need a bigger size.

That looks awful.   Does this look OK?   It looks fine.   It doesn't suit me.

The zip's broken.   I've just split my jeans.   Where did you get those?

Vous avez ça d'une autre couleur?

Do you have this in another colour?[1]

Je peux avoir une épingle de sûreté?

Could I have a safety pin?

clothes	les vêtements	a small size	une petite taille
shirt	une chemise		
T-shirt	un tee-shirt	a medium size	une taille moyenne
vest top	un débardeur		
sweatshirt	un sweat-shirt	a large size	une grande taille
jumper	un pull		
dress	une robe	too big	trop grand/grande
skirt	une jupe		
miniskirt	une mini-jupe	smaller	plus petit/petite
leggings	des jambières		
trousers	un pantalon	long	long/longue
shorts	un short	short	court/courte
track suit	un survêtement	tight	serré/serrée
top	le haut	baggy	large
bottom	le bas	fashion	la mode
trainers	des baskets	style	un style
shoes	des chaussures	look	un look
sandals	des sandales	fashionable	à la mode
boots	des bottes	trendy, cool	branché/branchée*
cowboy boots	des santiags		
		second-hand	d'occasion
braces	des bretelles	out-of-date	démodé/démodée
belt	une ceinture		
(bomber) jacket	un blouson	untrendy	ringard/ringarde*
boxer shorts	un caleçon	smart	chic
bra	un soutien-gorge	dressy	habillé/habillée
knickers	un slip	scruffy	crado*
tights	un collant	fun	chouette*
socks	des chaussettes	sale	soldes
swimsuit, trunks	un maillot (de bain)	changing room	cabine d'essayage

On peut venir en jean?

Je peux emprunter ta veste?

J'apporte mon maillot?

Are jeans all right?   Can I borrow your jacket?   Shall I bring my swimming stuff?

[1]See page 54 for a list of colours.

Music

Où est-ce que je peux acheter des disques?

Where's a good place to buy records?

Vous avez un rayon jazz?

Vous avez ça en cassette?

Do you have a jazz section?   Do you have this on cassette?

Types of music

This list includes music you're likely to hear in France. For other types of music, try using the English word as the names are often the same.

house music	la house music
heavy metal	le heavy metal
hard rock	le hard-rock
rock	le rock
punk	le punk
reggae	le reggae
funk	la musique funk
soul	la musique soul
African music	la musique africaine
jazz rock	le jazz-rock
rock & roll	le rock'n'roll
jazz	le jazz
blues	le blues
folk	le folk
pop	la musique pop
dance, disco	le disco
slow dances	les slows
classical	la musique classique

Can I put some music on?	Je peux mettre de la musique?
I listen to (lots of)...	J'écoute (beaucoup de)...
I've never heard any...	Je n'ai jamais entendu de...
Turn it up.	Plus fort.
It's too loud.	C'est trop fort.
Turn it down.	Baisse le volume.
Can you tape this for me?	Tu peux m'enregistrer ça?
music	la musique
record shop	un magasin de disques, un disquaire
radio	la radio
radio-cassette player	un lecteur radio-cassette
record-player	un tourne-disque
hi-fi	une chaîne hi-fi
Walkman†, personal stereo	un baladeur
headphones	des écouteurs
(radio) station	une station
single	un 45 (quarante-cinq) tours
album	un album, un 33 (trente-trois) tours
compact disc	un disque compact
a blank tape	une cassette vierge
music/pop video	un clip

Quel genre de musique tu aimes?

Ils sont nuls.

What kind of music do you like?   They're useless.

†A Walkman is a Sony product.

C'est de qui?	Tu as vu la vidéo?
Who's this by?	Have you seen the video?

Je peux emprunter cet album?
Can I borrow this album?

track	un morceau
song	une chanson
lyrics	les paroles
tune, melody	un air
rhythm, beat	le rythme
live	en direct
group, band	un groupe, un orchestre
orchestra	un orchestre
solo	en solo
singer	un chanteur/ une chanteuse
accompaniment, backup	l'accompagnement
fan	un fan
tour	une tournée
concert, gig	un concert
charts	le hit-parade
the Top 50[1]	le Top 50 (cinquante)
number one	le numéro un
hit	un tube
latest	dernier/dernière
new	nouveau/nouvelle
50's music	la musique des années 50
retro	rétro

Playing an instrument

Do you play an instrument?	Tu joues d'un instrument?
I play the guitar.	Je joue de la guitare.
I'm learning the drums.	J'apprends la batterie.
I play in a band.	Je joue dans un groupe.
I sing in a band.	Je chante dans un groupe.

instrument	un instrument
piano	le piano
keyboards	le clavier
drum machine	la boîte à rythmes
electric guitar	la guitare électrique
bass (guitar)	la guitare basse
saxophone	le saxophone
trumpet	la trompette
harmonica	l'harmonica
accordion	l'accordéon
violin	le violon
flute	la flûte
choir	une chorale

Tu as écouté le dernier trente-trois tours?	Il est génial.
Have you heard the latest album?	It's brilliant.

[1]The most common pop chart in France is the Top 50.

Going out: making arrangements, sightseeing

Making arrangements

What are we doing?	Have you got any ideas?

Shall we do something tonight?	I can't, I'm busy.[1]

Do you know a good place to...	Tu connais un endroit bien pour...	Can I get a ticket in advance?	Je peux prendre un billet à l'avance?
go dancing?	aller danser?	ticket office	le guichet
listen to music?	écouter de la musique?	student ticket	un billet étudiant
eat?	aller manger?	performance, film showing	une séance
go for a drink?	aller prendre un pot?	What time does it...	A quelle heure ça...
entertainment guide, listing	un programme des spectacles	start?[2]	commence?
nightclub, club	une boîte (de nuit)	finish?	finit?
disco	une boîte, une discothèque	open?	ouvre?
		close?	ferme?
party	une fête, une boum	today	aujourd'hui
picnic	un pique-nique	tonight	ce soir
show, entertainment	un spectacle	tomorrow	demain
(to the) cinema	(au) cinéma	day after tomorrow	après-demain
ballet	un ballet	(in the) morning	le matin
opera	un opéra	(in the) afternoon	l'après-midi
in town	en ville	(in the) evening	le soir
at X's place	chez X	this week	cette semaine
on the beach	à la plage	next week	la semaine prochaine

Sightseeing

What is there to see here?	Qu'est-ce qu'il y a à voir ici?	castle	un château
guide book	un guide	tower	une tour
tour	une visite	city walls	les remparts
region	la région	ruins	des ruines
countryside	la campagne	caves	des grottes
mountains	la montagne	amusement arcade	une galerie de jeux
lake	le lac	theme park	un parc d'attractions
river	la rivière	festival	une fête, un festival
coast	la côte	village dance	un bal populaire
museum	un musée	fireworks	un feu d'artifice
art gallery	un musée d'art	sound and light show[3]	un spectacle son et lumière
exhibition	une exposition	wine tasting	dégustation de vin
craft exhibition	exposition artisanale	interesting	intéressant/intéressante
the old town	la vieille ville	dull, boring	ennuyeux/ennuyeuse
cathedral	la cathédrale	beautiful	beau/belle
church	une église		

30 [1]Say Je suis prise if you're a girl. [2]See page 54 for days, dates and time. [3]These are outdoor shows at castles and other historic sites.

Où est-ce qu'on se retrouve?

A quelle heure?

| Where shall we meet? | What time? |

On se voit devant la fontaine.

See you at the fountain.

Deciding what to do

Qu'est-ce que tu veux faire?

Si on allait en boîte?

Qui est-ce qui joue au Jazz Bar?

| What do you want to do? | Let's go to a nightclub. | Who's playing at the Jazz Bar? |

On passe un bon film quelque part?

Qu'est-ce qui passe?

Je ne veux rien faire.

| What's on? | Are there any good films on? | I don't want to do anything. |

Fact file

If you want to find out what to visit, go to the tourist office (see page 4). Here you will get free maps, town plans and leaflets.

For what's on in Paris, look at *Pariscope* (a listings magazine), local English language magazines, or posters in *métro* stations or on *colonnes Morris* (round billboards in the street).

Films are often in *version originale* or *vo* (original language with subtitles). Student discounts are common.

Films, TV, books etc.

Films and TV

Books, magazines etc.

Je l'ai déjà vu.
I've already seen it.

C'est avec qui?
Who's in it?

cinema	le cinéma
film soc/club	un ciné-club, une cinémathèque
theatre	le théâtre
library	une bibliothèque
film, movie	un film
play	une pièce
book	un livre, un bouquin
magazine	un magazine
comic	une BD, une bande dessinée
novel	un roman
poetry	la poésie
author	l'auteur
director (film)	le réalisateur/la réalisatrice
cast	les acteurs
actor/actress	l'acteur/l'actrice
film buff	un mordu/une mordue du cinéma
production	une réalisation
plot	l'intrigue
story	l'histoire
set	le décor
special effects	les effets spéciaux
photography	la photographie
TV, telly	la télé
cable TV	la télé câblée
satellite TV	la télé par satellite
programme	le programme
channel	la chaîne
news	les informations
documentary	un documentaire
serial	un feuilleton
soap	un mélo
ads	la pub
dubbed	doublé/doublée
in English	en anglais
with subtitles	sous-titré/titrée

well known	très connu/connue
award-winning	primé/primée
fringe	d'avant-garde, expérimental
block buster	une super-production
a classic	un classique
comedy	une comédie
thriller	un thriller
musical	une comédie musicale
horror film	un film d'épouvante
adventure story	une histoire d'aventure
war film	un film de guerre
a western	un western
detective film	un film policier
sci-fi	la science-fiction
suspense	le suspense
sex	le sexe
violence	la violence
political	politique
satirical	satirique
serious	sérieux/sérieuse
offbeat	original/originale
commercial	commercial/e
exciting, gripping	passionnant/ passionnante
over the top	exagéré/ exagérée
good	bon/bonne
OK, not bad	pas mauvais/ mauvaise
bad, lousy	mauvais
silly	bête
funny	drôle
fun	marrant/marrante
sad	triste
It's scary.	Ça fait peur.

J'ai étudié ce bouquin à l'école.
I did that book at school.

C'est rasoir.*
It's so boring.

C'est génial.
It's brilliant.

C'est de qui?
Who's it by?

33

Where are you from?   I'm English.   What about you?

Where do you live?   I live near York.   How long have you been here?

What are you doing in France?   What do you think of France?   Where are you staying?

What's your name?	Jo.	How old are you?	I'm seventeen.

Are you alone?	No, I'm travelling with friends.	Have you got any sisters?

I'm English.[1]	Je suis anglais/anglaise.	your	ton/ta/tes[2]
My family is from...[1]	Ma famille vient de...	family	la famille
I've been here for two weeks.	Je suis ici depuis deux semaines.	parents	les parents
I'm on an exchange.	J'ai fait un échange.	father/mother	le père/la mère
I'm on holiday.	Je suis en vacances.	husband/wife	le mari/la femme
I'm staying with friends.	Je reste chez des amis.	boyfriend	le petit ami
I'm studying French.	J'étudie le français.	girlfriend	la petite amie
I'm travelling around.	Je voyage.	brother/sister	le frère/la soeur
I live ...	J'habite...	alone	seul/seule
in the country	à la campagne	single	célibataire
in a town	en ville	married	marié/mariée
in the suburbs	en banlieue	My parents are divorced.	Mes parents sont divorcés.
by the sea	au bord de la mer	My name is...	Je m'appelle...
in a house	dans une maison	surname	le nom de famille
in a flat	dans un appartement	nickname	le surnom
I live with...	J'habite chez...	my address	mon adresse
I don't live with...	Je n'habite pas chez...	My birthday is on the...[3]	Mon anniversaire est le...
my	mon/ma/mes[2]		

[1]Words for nationalities, countries and religions are on page 55. [2]Use *mon* with masculine, *ma* with feminine and *mes* with plural words. See page 52. [3]For days and dates, see page 54.

Other people

Gossip

Who's that?	Do you know Alain?	What's happened to Brigitte?	What's she like?	We get on OK.

friend	un ami/une amie	pretty	joli/jolie
mate, pal	un copain/une copine	good-looking	beau/belle
boy/girl	un garçon/une fille	OK (looks)	pas mal
bloke, guy	un type	not good-looking	pas beau/pas belle
someone	quelqu'un	ugly	laid/laide, moche*
has long hair	a les cheveux longs	a bit, a little	un peu
short hair	les cheveux courts	very	très, vachement*
curly hair	les cheveux frisés	so	tellement
straight hair	les cheveux raides	really	vraiment
has brown eyes	a les yeux marron	completely	complètement
he/she is...	il/elle est	nice, OK	sympa
tall	grand/grande	not nice, horrible	pas sympa
short	petit/petite	horrible, nasty	mauvais/mauvaise, vache*
fat	gros/grosse		
thin	mince	trendy, right on	branché/branchée*
is fair	est blond/blonde	old-fashioned, square	ringard/ringarde*
dark	brun/brune	clever	doué/douée

Making the first move

He's a good laugh.	I like him.	He's tall.	I can't stand her.	She's quite pretty.

thick	bête	cool	cool*
boring	rasoir*	a creep	un minable, un pauvre type
shy	timide		
mad, crazy	fou/folle, dingue*	an idiot, a prat	un crétin/une crétine
weird	bizarre	in a bad mood	de mauvaise humeur
lazy	paresseux/paresseuse	in a good mood	de bonne humeur
laid back	relax/relaxe*	angry, annoyed	fâché/fâchée
up-tight	coincé/coincée	depressed	déprimé/déprimée
mixed up, untogether	compliqué/compliquée	happy	heureux/heureuse
selfish	égoïste	Have you heard...?	Tu sais que...?
jealous	jaloux/jalouse	Brigitte is going out with Alain.	Brigitte sort avec Alain.
rude	grossier/grossière		
macho	macho	Luc got off with Sylvie.	Luc a une touche* avec Sylvie.
stuck up	snob		
sloaney[1], yuppie	BCBG (bon chic, bon genre), yuppie	He/she kissed me.	Il/elle m'a embrassé/e.
		They split up.	Ils ont cassé.
loaded, rich	friqué/friquée*	We had a row.	On s'est disputé.

[1]The term *BCBG* is the closest to "sloaney" but is sometimes used to mean something like "yuppie".

sport	un sport
match	un match
a game (of)	une partie (de)
doubles	double
singles	simple
race	une course
marathon	un marathon
championships	les championnats
Olympics	les Jeux olympiques
World cup	la Coupe du monde
club	un club
team	une équipe
referee	un arbitre
supporter	un supporter
training, practice	l'entraînement
a goal	un but
to lose	perdre
a draw	match nul
sports centre	le centre sportif
stadium	le stade
court	le court
indoor	couvert/couverte
outdoor	en plein air
ball (small)	la balle
ball (large)	le ballon
net	le filet
trainers	des chaussures de sport
tennis shoes	des tennis
tracksuit	un survêtement

once a week	une fois par semaine
twice a week	deux fois par semaine
I play...	Je joue au...
I don't play...	Je ne joue pas au...
tennis	tennis
squash	squash
badminton	badminton
football	football
American football	football américain
basketball	basket
volleyball	volley
table tennis	ping-pong
cricket	cricket
baseball	base-ball
I do, I go...	Je fais...
I don't do/go...	Je ne fais pas de...[1]
judo	du judo
karate	du karaté
aerobics	de l'aérobic
jogging	du jogging
running	de la course à pied
weight-training	des poids et haltères
body-building	de la musculation
keep-fit	de l'entretien
bowling	du bowling
dancing	de la danse

How do you play this?	Comment on joue à ça?
What are the rules?	Quelles sont les règles?
Throw it to me.	Lance-le moi.
Catch!	Attrape!
In!/Out!	In!/Out!
You're cheating!	Tu triches!
What team do you support?	Tu es pour quelle équipe?
Is there a match we could go to?	Il y a un match qu'on pourrait aller voir?
Who won?	Qui a gagné?

Fact file

Football, tennis, basketball and volleyball are popular games. Rugby is played a lot in the south and south west. Cycling is very popular, and the biggest spectator event is the annual *Tour de France*, a three week cycle race. In the south particularly, people of all ages play *boules* or *pétanque*[2] (both played with metal balls, often on a patch of ground in the town square). Winter sports are very popular, with downhill skiing in the Alps and Pyrenees, but also cross-country in the Jura, Vosges and Massif Central.

[1] When saying *Je ne fais pas*, don't use *du, de la* or *de l'*. Use *de* instead, e.g. *je ne fais pas de judo* [2] *Pétanque* is a type of *boules* game originally played in Provence.

I like...	J'aime...
I don't like...	Je n'aime pas...
I love...	J'adore...
I prefer...	Je préfère...
swimming	la natation
(scuba) diving	la plongée
sunbathing	me faire bronzer
sailing	faire de la voile
surfing	le surf
water skiing	le ski nautique
canoeing	faire du canoë
rowing	faire de l'aviron
boat	un bateau
surfboard	une planche de surf
windsurfer	une planche à voile
boom	la bôme
mast	le mât
sail	la voile
sea	la mer
beach	la plage
swimming pool	la piscine
in the sun	au soleil
in the shade	à l'ombre
goggles	des lunettes de plongée
mask	un masque
snorkel	un tuba
flippers	des palmes
wetsuit	une combinaison de plongée
life jacket	un gilet de sauvetage
fishing	la pêche
rod	la canne à pêche

cycling	le cyclisme
racing bike	un vélo de course
mountain bike	un vélo tout terrain
touring bike	un vélo de randonnée
BMX	un BMX
horse riding	l'équitation
horse	un cheval
walking, hiking	la marche à pied
footpath	un chemin (de randonnée)
skate board	un skateboard
skateboarding	faire du skateboard
roller skating	le patin à roulettes
ice skating	le patin à glace
ice rink	une patinoire
skates	des patins
skiing	le ski
cross-country skiing	le ski de fond
ski run	une piste de ski
ski pass	un forfait
ski lifts	remontées mécaniques
chair lift	le télésiège
drag lift	le téléski, le tire-fesses*
skis	des skis
boots	des chaussures de ski
bindings	les fixations
ski goggles	des lunettes de ski
snow	la neige

[1] Another term for (rock) climbing is l'escalade.

Studying

What do you do?	Where are you studying?	What sort of college is it?
What time do you finish?	Do you have a lot of work?	Yes loads.

I'm a student.	*Je suis étudiant/ étudiante.*	Spanish	*l'espagnol*
I'm still at school.	*Je vais encore à l'école.*	Italian	*l'italien*
I want to do...	*J'aimerais faire du/de la/de l'/ des...*	German	*l'allemand*
		Russian	*le russe*
I do...	*Je fais du/de la/de l'/ des...* [1]	literature	*la littérature*
		philosophy	*la philosophie, la philo*
computing	*l'informatique*	sociology	*la sociologie*
maths	*les maths*	religious studies	*l'instruction religieuse*
physics	*la physique*	general studies	*l'éducation civique*
chemistry	*la chimie*	art	*le dessin*
biology	*la biologie*	drama	*le théâtre*
natural sciences	*les sciences naturelles, sciences nat*	needlework	*la couture*
		woodwork	*la menuiserie-ébénisterie*
geography	*la géographie*		
history	*l'histoire*	metalwork	*le travail des métaux*
economics	*l'économie*	technical drawing	*le dessin industriel*
business studies	*les études commerciales*	PE	*la gym*
languages	*les langues*	school	*une école, un bahut**
French	*le français*	mixed	*mixte*
English	*l'anglais*	boarding school	*un internat*

[1]*Du* + masculine words, *de la* + feminine words, *de l'* + words beginning with a vowel, *des* + plural words. See page 51.

Fact file: the French system

Types of schools and colleges:[2]

–un collège (comprehensive type school for first four years of secondary school)

–un lycée d'enseignement professionnel (secondary school with vocational bias)

–un lycée (similar to a grammar school)

–un IUT or Institut Universitaire de Technologie (polytechnic)

–une université, une faculté often shortened to fac (university)

–les Hautes Ecoles (élite universities with entry by concours, competitive exams).

School is compulsory until 16. Most schools are mixed and uniform is rare. Summer holidays go from late June to early September. Schools employ surveillants or pions* to keep discipline. Secondary school starts at about 11 in Sixième and goes up to Première and Terminale[3]. At about 16, most pupils get the Brevet certificate, based on average marks. Many pupils go on to take the CAP or BEP (vocational exams), the BT (more technological), or Bac – short for Baccalauréat – which gives access to universities. Le service militaire (national service) is compulsory for men at 19 but can be deferred while studying.

private school	un collège privé	continual assessment	le contrôle continu
term	un trimestre	mark, grade	la note
during term time	pendant le trimestre		
holidays	les vacances	teacher	le professeur, le/la prof
beginning of term	la rentrée	lecturer	le prof, le maître
uniform	un uniforme		de conférences
school club	un club, un foyer	(language) assistant	l'assistant/l'assistante
form leader	le délégué/la déléguée	good	bon/bonne
	de classe	bad	mauvais/mauvaise
lesson, lecture	un cours	easy going	pas strict, sympa
tuition, private	des cours particuliers,	strict	strict/stricte sévère
lessons	soutien	discipline	la discipline
homework	des devoirs		
essay	une dissertation	to repeat (a year)	redoubler
translation	une traduction	expelled	renvoyé/renvoyée
project	un projet	to skip a lesson	sauter un cours
revision	la révision	to skive, to bunk off	faire l'école
test	un contrôle		buissonnière
oral test	un oral		
oral	oral/orale	a grant	une bourse
written	écrit/écrite	free	gratuit/gratuite
presentation	un exposé		

[2]The equivalents in brackets are only approximate. [3]Literally, these mean sixth, first and final forms.

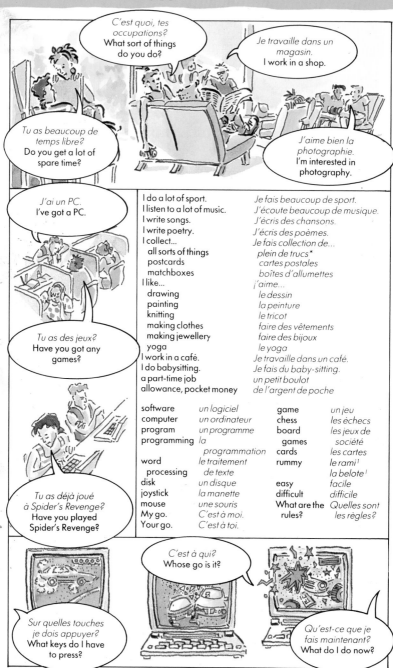

C'est quoi, tes occupations?
What sort of things do you do?

Je travaille dans un magasin.
I work in a shop.

Tu as beaucoup de temps libre?
Do you get a lot of spare time?

J'aime bien la photographie.
I'm interested in photography.

J'ai un PC.
I've got a PC.

Tu as des jeux?
Have you got any games?

Tu as déjà joué à Spider's Revenge?
Have you played Spider's Revenge?

C'est à qui?
Whose go is it?

Sur quelles touches je dois appuyer?
What keys do I have to press?

Qu'est-ce que je fais maintenant?
What do I do now?

I do a lot of sport.	Je fais beaucoup de sport.
I listen to a lot of music.	J'écoute beaucoup de musique.
I write songs.	J'écris des chansons.
I write poetry.	J'écris des poèmes.
I collect...	Je fais collection de...
all sorts of things	plein de trucs*
postcards	cartes postales
matchboxes	boîtes d'allumettes
I like...	j'aime...
drawing	le dessin
painting	la peinture
knitting	le tricot
making clothes	faire des vêtements
making jewellery	faire des bijoux
yoga	le yoga
I work in a café.	Je travaille dans un café.
I do babysitting.	Je fais du baby-sitting.
a part-time job	un petit boulot
allowance, pocket money	de l'argent de poche

software	un logiciel	game	un jeu
computer	un ordinateur	chess	les échecs
program	un programme	board games	les jeux de société
programming	la programmation	cards	les cartes
word processing	le traitement de texte	rummy	le rami[1] la belote[1]
disk	un disque	easy	facile
joystick	la manette	difficult	difficile
mouse	une souris	What are the rules?	Quelles sont les règles?
My go.	C'est à moi.		
Your go.	C'est à toi.		

44 [1]Popular card games in France. [2]Countries are listed on page 55. *Aller au* + (m) country names, *aux* + plural, *en* + (f) or names that start with a vowel.

Plans

What do you want to do later?	Tu veux faire quoi, plus tard?
When I finish...	Quand j'aurai fini...
One day...	Un jour...
I want...	Je voudrais...
to travel	voyager
to go to...[2]	aller au/aux/en...[2]
to live/work abroad	habiter/travailler à l'étranger
to have a career	faire une carrière
to get a good job	trouver un bon boulot
to get my qualifications	obtenir mes diplômes
to carry on studying	poursuivre mes études
I want to be a...	Je voudrais être...
I don't want to be a...	Je ne voudrais pas être...

> Je voudrais faire le tour du monde.
> I want to go round the world.

> Moi aussi.
> So do I.

Issues

What do you think about...?	Qu'est-ce que tu penses de...?	war	la guerre
I don't know much about...	Je ne sais pas grand chose sur...	terrorism	le terrorisme
Can you explain...?	Tu peux expliquer...?	environment	l'environnement
I think...	Je pense...	conservation	la conservation
I believe in...	Je crois à...	ecology	l'écologie
I'm for, I support...	Je suis pour...	ozone layer	la couche d'ozone
I belong to...	J'appartiens à...	animals	les bêtes
I don't believe in...	Je ne crois pas à...	plants	les plantes
I'm against...	Je suis contre...	trees	les arbres
I feel angry about (pollution).	(La pollution), ça me met en colère.	deforestation	le déboisement
I agree.	Je suis d'accord.	acid rain	les pluies acides
You're right.	Tu as raison.	pollution	la pollution
I don't agree.	Je ne suis pas d'accord.	nuclear power	l'énergie nucléaire
the future	l'avenir	recycling	le recyclage
(in) the past	(dans) le passé	politics	la politique
now, nowadays	de nos jours, maintenant	government	le gouvernement
important	important/importante	democratic	démocratique
		elections	des élections
		party	un parti
religion	la religion	revolution	une révolution
god	dieu	the left	la gauche
human rights	les droits de l'homme	the right	la droite
gay	gay, homo	fascist	fasciste
feminist	féministe	communist	communiste
abortion	l'avortement	socialist	socialiste
drugs	les drogues	left-wing	gauchiste
drug addict	un drogué/une droguée	greens, green movement	les verts, les écologistes
Aids	le Sida	conservative	conservateur
rich, well-off	riche	reactionary	réactionnaire, réac *
poor	pauvre	militant	militant/militante
unemployment	le chômage	politically active, committed	engagé/engagée
Third World	le Tiers-Monde	a charity	une oeuvre de bienfaisance
peace	la paix		
nuclear disarmament	le désarmement nucléaire	march, demo	une manifestation, une manif *

Illness, problems[1] and emergencies

doctor	le docteur, le médecin
woman doctor	une femme docteur
dentist	le dentiste
optician	l'opticien
chemist[2]	la pharmacie
pill[2]	un cachet, une pilule
suppository[3]	un suppositoire
injection	une piqûre
I'm allergic	Je suis allergique
to antibiotics	aux antibiotiques
to some medicines	à certains médicaments
I have...	J'ai...
food poisoning	un empoisonnement alimentaire
diarrhoea	la diarrhée
cramp	une crampe
sunstroke	un coup de soleil
a headache	mal à la tête
a stomach ache	mal au ventre
my period	mes règles
an infection	une infection
a sore throat	mal à la gorge
a cold	un rhume
hayfever	le rhume des foins
flu	la grippe
a toothache	mal aux dents
a temperature	de la température
a hangover	la gueule de bois
He/she's had too much to drink.	Il/elle a trop bu.
I feel dizzy.	J'ai la tête qui tourne.
I'm constipated.	Je suis constipé/constipée.
I've been stung by a wasp.	J'ai été piqué/e par une guêpe.
I've got mosquito bites.	J'ai été piqué/e par des moustiques.
It hurts a lot.	Ça fait très mal.
It hurts a little.	Ça fait un peu mal.
I've cut myself.	Je me suis coupé/coupée.
I think I've broken my...	Je crois que je me suis cassé...
My ... hurts.	J'ai mal au/à la/à l'...[4]
eye	l'oeil
nose	le nez
mouth	la bouche
ear	l'oreille
chest	la poitrine
arm	le bras
elbow	le coude
hand	la main
wrist	le poignet
finger	le doigt
leg	la jambe
knee	le genou
ankle	la cheville
foot	le pied
bottom	le derrière
back	le dos
skin	la peau
muscle	le muscle

46 [1]For problems not listed here, try asking *Vous avez un dictionnaire?* (Do you have a dictionary?) [2]Everyday things like plasters and aspirin are on page 24. [3]These are often

Problems

> J'ai perdu un verre de contact.
> I've lost my contact lens.

> On m'a volé mes affaires.
> Someone's stolen my things.

> J'ai cassé mes lunettes.
> I've broken my glasses.

> Je n'ai pas vu ce qui s'est passé.
> I didn't see what happened.

wallet	mon portefeuille	There's no water/ power	Il n'y a pas d'eau/de courant.
handbag	mon sac à main		
my things	mes affaires	I'm lost.	Je suis perdu/ perdue.
my papers	mes papiers		
my passport	mon passeport	I'm in trouble.	J'ai des ennuis.
my key	ma clé	I'm scared.	J'ai peur.
all my money	tout mon argent	I need to talk to someone.	Il faut que je parle à quelqu'un.
lost property	objets perdus		
Can you keep an eye on my things?	Vous pouvez surveiller mes affaires?	I don't know what to do...	Je ne sais pas quoi faire...
Has anyone seen...?	Quelqu'un a vu...?	I don't want to cause trouble, but...	Je ne veux pas faire d'ennuis, mais...
Please don't smoke.	Ça vous ennuierait de ne pas fumer?		
Where's the socket?	Où est la prise?	A man's following me.	Il y a un homme qui me suit.
It doesn't work.	Ça ne marche pas.		

Fact file

In France everyone has to carry their identity card, so keep your passport with you. Don't be surprised if you are asked to show your *papiers* (documents, ID).

For minor health problems or first aid treatment go to a chemist. For something more serious go to a doctor or the casualty department of the local hospital. In each case you should expect to pay. You should be able to claim back expenses on insurance[5], but hang on to all the paperwork.

Watch out for these signs: *Sortie de secours* (emergency exit); *Attention* (beware); *Chien méchant* (ferocious dog); *Défense d'entrer* (keep out, no entry); *Propriété privée* (private property); *Danger* (danger); *Eau potable* (drinking water); *Eau non potable* (not drinking water); *Camping sauvage interdit* (no unauthorised camping); *Baignade interdite* (no swimming).

Emergencies

Emergency phone numbers: police, 17; fire brigade, 18; ambulance, 17 or 18 (from 1992, call 112 for all three services). For very serious problems, contact the closest *Consulat Britannique* (British Consulate). Find the number in the directory.

There's been an accident.	Il vient d'y avoir un accident.
Help!	Au secours!
Fire!	Au feu!
Please call...	S'il vous plaît, appelez...
an ambulance	une ambulance
the police	la police
the fire brigade	les pompiers
the lifeguard	le maître-nageur
hospital	l'hôpital
casualty department	le service des urgences
police station	le commissariat de police

prescribed in France. [4]*Au* + (m) words, *à la* + (f) words, *à l'* + words beginning with a vowel. See page 51. [5]British passport holders can use an E111 form – available from the DSS.

The French that people use every day, especially amongst friends, is different in lots of ways from correct textbook French. As in English, people use slang and have alternative ways of saying things. They also leave out bits of words (e.g. in English "I do not know" can end up sounding like "I dunno"). This book has included informal French and slang words where appropriate, but these two pages list a few of the most common words and phrases.

When using colloquial language it is easy to sound off-hand or even rude without meaning to. This is especially true for slang words, so here as in the rest of the book a single asterisk after a word shows it is mild slang, but two asterisks show it can be quite rude and it is safest not to experiment with it.

Contractions and alternative pronunciations

I	j'* (je)[1]
I don't know	j'sais pas* (je ne sais pas)
I haven't	j'ai pas* (je n'ai pas)
you have	t'as* (tu as)
you are	t'es* (tu es)
there is/are	y a* (il y a)
yes	ouais* (oui)
well	ben*, eh ben* (bien, eh bien)

Abbreviations

nice, friendly	sympa (sympathique)
mad, crazy, keen	fana (fanatique)
ecologist	un écolo (écologiste)
intellectual	un intello (intellectuel)
teacher	un prof (professeur)
in the morning	du mat' (du matin)
cinema	le ciné (cinéma)
test	une interro (interrogation)
flat	un appart' (appartement)

American and English imports

un boss; cool; flipper (to flip); un job; le look; non-stop; un scoop; sexy; le show-biz; un spot (a commercial, an ad); le stress...

Fillers and exclamations

OK	OK, bien
right	bon, alors
well	eh bien
actually, in fact	en fait
by the way	au fait
damn	mince*
shoot, damn	zut*, zut* alors

Slang

very	hyper, super, vachement*
great, brilliant, classic	génial/géniale, super, terrible, d'enfer, chouette*, dément/démente
lousy, bad, disgusting	moche, dégueulasse**, infect/infecte
boring	emmerdant/emmerdante**
irritating, annoying	énervant/énervante, casse-pieds*
funny	marrant/marrante,
crazy, barmy, whacky	dingue*, taré/tarée*, sonné/sonnée*, timbré/timbrée*,
lucky	verni/vernie*
broke	fauché/fauchée*
guy, bloke	un type*, un mec*
girl	une nana**, une minette*
friend, mate	un pote*
boyfriend	un Jules**
kid	un/une gosse, un/une môme*
policeman	un flic*
money, dough	les sous, le pognon*, le fric*, le blé*, les ronds*
francs	balles*, e.g. 100 balles*
clothes	les fringues*
car	la bagnole*
food, grub	la bouffe*
cinema	le cinoche*
school	le bahut*
school, company	la boîte*
room	la piaule*
joke	une blague
problem	un pépin*
to have fun	se marrer
to understand, get it	piger*
to talk rubbish	baratiner*
to chat up	baratiner*, draguer**
to eat	bouffer*
to steal, nick	piquer*
to throw out	virer
to break down, freak out	craquer
to fail, fall through	foirer*
to be careful	faire gaffe*
to be on top form	avoir une pêche d'enfer*
to be full of beans	avoir la frite*
to work	bosser*
It's a turn-on.	C'est le pied.*
You're joking.	Tu blagues.*
You're getting on my nerves.	Tu m'énerves.
Leave me alone.	Fiche-moi la paix.**
I don't care.	Je m'en fiche.* Je m'en fous.**

[1]The contracted je sounds like a soft "sh", e.g. sh peux for je peux (I can).

French pronunciation

To pronounce French well you need the help of a French speaker or language tapes, but these general points will help. Bear in mind that there are exceptions and regional variations.

Vowel sounds

a sounds like "a" in cat.
e, eu and *oe* sound a bit like "u" in "fur". At the end of a word, *e* is silent.
é sounds like "a" in "late", but a bit clipped.
è, ê and *ai* sound like "ai" in "air".
i sounds like "i" in machine but clipped.
o sounds like "o" in soft.
ô, au, and *eau* sound like "au" in "autumn".
u is a sharp "u" sound. Round your lips to say "oo", try to say "ee", and you will be close.
oi sounds like "wa" in "wagon".
ou sounds like "oo" in "moody".
ui sounds like "wee" in "week".

Nasal sounds

French has some slightly nasal sounds in which the "n" or "m" are barely sounded:
an and *en* are a bit like "aun" in "aunt".
am and *em* (when they precede "p" or "b") sound like *an/en* but with a hint of an "m".
in (when it precedes a consonant or is on the end of a word) and *ain* sound a bit like "an" in "can".
im (when it precedes "p" or "b") sounds like *in/ain* but with a hint of an "m".
on is a bit like "on" in "song".
un (on end of a word or before a consonant) is a bit like "an" in "an apple".

Consonants

c is hard as in "cat" except before "i" or "e" or with a cedilla: *ç*. Then it is like "s" in "sun".
ch sounds like "sh" in "shoe".
g is like "g" in "go" except before "e" or "i". Then it is like the "j" sound in "measure".
gn is like the "nio" sound in "onion".
h is never pronounced.
j is like a soft *g*, see above.
ll when it follows "i" is like "y" in "young".
ail on the end of a word is like "y" in "sky".
qu is the same as a hard *c* (the "u" is silent).
r is made in the back of the throat.
s is like "z" in "zoo", and *ss* or *s* at the start of a word is like "s" in "soap".
Consonants on ends of words are usually silent unless an "e" comes after. On ends of words *er, et* and *ez* usually sound like *é*.

The alphabet in French

Applying the points above, this is how you say the alphabet: *A, Bé, Çé, Dé, Eu, èFe, G = jé, acHe, I, Ji, Ka, èLe, èMe, èNe, O, Pé, Quu, èRe, èSse, Té, U, Vé, W = double-vé, iXe, Y = i-grèque, Zède.*

How French works

Nouns

All French nouns are either masculine (m) or feminine (f).

For a few nouns the gender is obvious, e.g. *le garçon* (boy) is masculine and *la fille* (girl) is feminine. For most nouns the gender seems random, e.g. *le tronc* (trunk) is masculine and *la branche* (branch) is feminine. Some nouns can be either gender, e.g. *le/la touriste* (tourist m/f) and some have two forms, e.g. *l'étudiant/l'étudiante* (student m/f).

The article (the word for "the" or "a") shows the gender of the noun:
with masculine nouns, "the" is *le*, e.g. *le train* (the train) and "a" is *un*, e.g. *un train* (a train);
with feminine nouns, "the" is *la*, e.g. *la boîte* (the box) and "a" is *une*, e.g. *une boîte* (a box);
with nouns that begin with a vowel[1], "the" is always *l'*, e.g. *l'avion* (the plane) or *l'étoile* (the star). "A" is still *un* or *une*, e.g. *un avion* (a plane) or *une étoile* (a star).

Sometimes French uses an article where English doesn't, e.g. *J'aime le thé* (I like tea).

To help you get articles right, the book gives nouns with the article most likely to be useful in the context, and the Index makes genders clear by listing nouns with *le* or *la*, or adding (m) or (f) after those that begin with a vowel.

Don't worry if you muddle up *le* and *la*, you will still be understood. It is worth knowing the gender of nouns since other words, particularly adjectives, change to match them. If you're learning a noun, learn it with *le* or *la* – or *un* or *une* for nouns that begin with a vowel.
A useful tip is that many nouns ending in "e" are feminine.

Plurals

In the plural, the French for "the" is *les*, e.g. *les trains* (the trains).

In English "some" (the plural for "a") is often left out. In French *un* or *une* becomes *des* in the plural and is always used, e.g. *Il y a des types qui* ... (There are blokes who...)

To make a noun plural, add "s", e.g. *deux trains* (two trains). For some nouns you add "x", e.g. *deux gâteaux* (two cakes).

[1]"The" is also *l'* with some nouns that begin with "h", e.g. *l'heure* (the hour), *l'homme* (the man), *l'horloge* (the clock).

De, du, de la, de l', des (any, some)

When talking about things like butter or water, English uses "any", "some" or no article, e.g. Is there any butter left? I want some butter. There's water in the jug.

French has a special article that is always used in these cases, de + "the", but de + le are contracted to du and de +les to des so you use:

du + (m) noun, e.g. *Tu veux du café?* (Would you like some coffee?);
de la + (f) noun, e.g. *Tu as de la musique punk?* (Do you have any punk music?);
de l' + nouns beginning with a vowel, e.g. *Tu veux de l'eau gazeuse?* (Do you want any fizzy water?);
des + plural nouns, e.g. *Tu veux des frites?* (Do you want some chips?).

In negative sentences simply use de + noun, or d' before a vowel, e.g. *Je ne veux pas de café/d'eau* (I don't want any coffee/water).

De (of)

In French "of" is *de*. It works in the same way as *de* meaning "any, some": with (m) nouns use *du*, e.g. *la couleur du mur* (the colour of the wall), and so on.

French uses "of" to show possession where English does not, e.g. *le pull de Paul* (Paul's jumper, literally "the jumper of Paul").

Au, à la, à l', aux (to, at)

The French for "to" and "at" is *à*. With *le* and *les*, *à* contracts to *au* and *aux* so you use:
au + (m) nouns, e.g. *Je vais au ciné* (I'm going to the cinema);
à la + (f) nouns, e.g. *Je suis à la gare* (I'm at the station);
à l' + nouns that begin with a vowel, e.g. *Je suis à l'aéroport* (I'm at the airport);
aux + plural nouns, e.g. *Je vais aux Etats-Unis* (I'm going to the States).

Ceci, cela, ça (this, that)

"This" is *ceci*, "that" is *cela*, but both are shortened to *ça* in everyday French, e.g. *Je voudrais ça* (I'd like this/that).

Celui-ci and *celle-ci* are the (m) and (f) forms for "this one" and *celui-là* and *celle-là* are the (m) and (f) forms for "that one".

Ce, cette, cet, ces (this, that)

Used as an adjective, "this" and "that" are:
ce + (m) nouns, e.g. *ce type* (this bloke);
cette + (f) nouns, e.g. *cette fille* (this girl);

cet + nouns beginning with a vowel, e.g. *cet idiot* (that idiot);
ces + plural nouns, e.g. *ces filles* (those girls).

Adjectives

In French, many adjectives agree with the noun they refer to – they change when used with a feminine or plural noun.

Many add an "e" on the end when used with a (f) noun. The "e" also changes the sound of the word as it means you pronounce the consonant, e.g. *vert* (green) with a silent "t" becomes *verte* with a voiced "t": *un pull vert* (a green jumper), *une porte verte* (a green door).

Most adjectives that end in a vowel add an extra "e" but sound the same, e.g. *bleu/bleue*. In this book, adjectives that change are given twice, (m) form followed by (f) form, e.g. *vert/verte* (green). Some adjectives don't change, e.g. any that end in "e" like *sympathique* (nice).

In the plural, most adjectives add an "s", e.g. *des pulls verts* (green jumpers), *des portes vertes* (green doors).

Most adjectives come after the noun but some common ones usually come before, e.g.:

beautiful	beau/belle	young	jeune
good	bon/bonne	pretty	joli/jolie
nice, kind	gentil/ gentille	long	long/longue
big, tall	grand/ grande	bad	mauvais/ mauvaise
fat, big	gros/ grosse	small, short	petit/ petite
		old	vieux/vieille

Making comparisons

To make a comparison, put the following words in front of the adjective:
plus (more, ...er), e.g. *plus important* (more important), *plus gros* (fatter);
moins (less), e.g. *moins gros* (less fat);
aussi (as), e.g *aussi gros* (as fat);
le plus/la plus (the most, the ...est), e.g. *le plus important* (the most important).

plus ... que (more ... than, ...er ... than), e.g. *Il est plus grand que Joe* (He's taller than Joe);
moins que (less ... than), e.g. *Elle est moins grande que lui* (She's less tall than him);
aussi ... que (as ... as), e.g. *Il est aussi maigre qu'elle* (He's as thin as her).
Que (than) shortens to *qu'* in front of a vowel.

There are some exceptions, e.g. *bon/bonne* (good), *meilleur/meilleure* (better), *le meilleur/la meilleure* (the best); *mauvais/ mauvaise* (bad), *pire* (worse), *le pire/la pire* (the worst).

My, your, his, her etc.

In French these words agree with the noun they relate to, e.g. *mon frère* (my brother), *ma soeur* (my sister), *mes parents* (my parents).

In front of	(m) noun	(f) noun	plural noun
my	mon	ma	mes
your	ton	ta	tes
his/her	son	sa	ses
our	notre	notre	nos
your	votre	votre	vos
their	leur	leur	leurs

Before a vowel or "h", use the (m) form, e.g. *mon écharpe* (my scarf) even though *écharpe* is (f).

I, you, he, she etc.

I	*je* or *j'*	*Je* shortens to *j'* in front of vowels, e.g. *j'aime* (I like).
you	*tu* or *vous*	Say *tu* to a friend or someone your own age or younger. Use *vous* when you talk to someone older, whether you know them or not. If in doubt, use *vous*. Saying *tu* to someone who doesn't expect it can be rude. *Vous* is also the plural form. Use it when speaking to more than one person.
he	*il*	
she	*elle*	
it	*il* or *elle*	There is no special word for "it". Since nouns are (m) or (f), you use "he" to refer to a male or (m) thing and "she" to refer to a female or (f) thing, e.g. *Le train? Il est en retard.* (The train? It's late) or *La gare? Elle est là-bas.* (The station? It's over there.)
we	*nous* or *on*	*Nous* means "we", e.g. *Nous sommes en retard* (We are late). People often use *on* instead as *nous* sounds formal. Like "one" in English, *on* takes the he/she form of the verb: *On est en retard* (We're late, literally "One is late").
they	*ils* or *elles*	*Ils* is used for males and (m) things, and *elles* for females and (f) things.

Me, you, him etc.

me	me	him/it	le	us	nous
you	te	her/it	la	you	vous
				them	les

In French these come before the verb, e.g. *Je le veux* (I want it).

Verbs

French verbs have more tenses (present, future etc.) than English verbs, but there are simple ways of getting by which are explained here.

Present tense

Many French verbs end in "er" in the infinitive[1], e.g. *regarder* (to watch) and follow the same pattern. Drop "er" and replace it with the ending you need:

I watch	je	regard e
you watch	tu	regard es
he/she/it/watches	il/elle	regard e
we watch	nous	regard ons
you watch	vous	regard ez
they watch	ils/elles	regard ent

French doesn't distinguish between the two English present tenses, e.g. I watch or I'm watching, so *je regarde* can mean either. Another tip is that verbs are easier than they look: many forms sound the same even though the spelling changes, e.g. *aime*, *aimes* and *aiment* all sound the same.

Useful irregular verbs

to be	être	to have (got)	avoir
I am	je suis	I have	j'ai
you are	tu es	you have	tu as
he/it is	il est	he/it has	il a
she/it is	elle est	she/it has	elle a
we are	nous sommes	we have	nous avons
you are	vous êtes	you have	vous avez
they are	ils sont elles sont	they have	ils ont elles ont

to want to	vouloir	to be able to	pouvoir
I want	je veux	I can	je peux
you want	tu veux	you can	tu peux
he/it wants	il veut	he/it can	il peut
she/it wants	elle veut	she/it can	elle peut
we want	nous voulons	we can	nous pouvons
you want	vous voulez	you can	vous pouvez
they want	ils/elles veulent	they can	ils/elles peuvent

to have to/must		devoir	
I have to/must		je dois	
you have to/must		tu dois	
he/it has to/must		il doit	
she/it has to/must		elle doit	
we have to/must		nous devons	
you have to/must		vous devez	
they have to/must		ils/elles doivent	

[1]The infinitive, e.g. "to read", "to like" is the form in which verbs are given in the Index and in dictionaries. Many French infinitives end in "er", and quite a few end in "ir".

The last three verbs are handy for making sentences like:

Je veux manger (I want to eat);
Je peux venir avec toi (I can come with you);
Je dois regarder la télé (I must watch TV).

The second verb is in the infinitive[1]. The Index lists verbs in this form, and many French infinitives can be spotted by their "er" or "ir" endings.

to go	*aller*	to come	*venir*
I go	*je vais*	I come	*je viens*
you go	*tu vas*	you come	*tu viens*
he/it goes	*il va*	he/it comes	*il vient*
she/it goes	*elle va*	she/it comes	*elle vient*
we go	*nous allons*	we come	*nous venons*
you go	*vous allez*	you come	*vous venez*
they go	*ils vont* *elles vont*	you come they come	*vous venez* *ils/elles viennent*

Talking about the future

There is a future tense in French, e.g. *Je regarderai la télé* (I shall watch TV) but it is easier to use the "going to" future: *Je vais regarder la télé* (I'm going to watch TV). For everyday use, this form is also more common. As in English, simply use the present of *aller* (to go) + an infinitive[1].

Talking about the past

The easiest way is to use the perfect tense, e.g. *j'ai regardé* which can mean "I watched" or "I have watched". You make the perfect with the present of *avoir* (to have) + the verb's past participle:
"er" verbs[1] change their ending to "é" in the past participle, e.g. *regarder* becomes *regardé* (they sound just the same);
"ir"[1] verbs change to "i", e.g. *dormir* becomes *dormi: il a dormi* (he slept/has slept).

Some verbs form the perfect tense with *être* (to be), e.g. *Il est allé* (he went/has been). Below are the most useful ones (past participles are also shown if they are not "er" or "ir" verbs):

to go	*aller*	to go home	*rentrer*
to arrive	*arriver*		
to go down	*descendre, descendu*	to go back	*retourner*
		to stay	*rester*
to become	*devenir, devenu*	to go out	*sortir*
		to fall	*tomber*
to go in	*entrer*	to come	*venir, venu*
to go up	*monter*		
to leave	*partir*		

The imperfect, or past, tense of "to be" and "to have" is also useful for talking about the past:

I was	*j'étais*	I had	*j'avais*
you were	*tu étais*	you had	*tu avais*
he/it was	*il était*	he/it had	*il avait*
she/it was	*elle était*	she/it had	*elle avait*
we were	*nous étions*	we had	*nous avions*
you were	*vous étiez*	you had	*vous aviez*
they were	*ils/elles étaient*	they had	*ils/elles avaient*

Negatives

To make a sentence negative, put *ne* and *pas* on either side of the verb, e.g. *je veux* (I want), *je ne veux pas* (I don't want) or *j'aime danser* (I like dancing), *je n'aime pas danser* (I don't like dancing).

In everyday, spoken French it is very common to drop the *ne*, e.g. *je veux pas* (I don't want).

Other useful negative words:
ne ... jamais (never), e.g. *Il ne veut jamais* (He never wants);
ne ... personne (nobody), e.g. *Je n'aime personne* (I don't like anybody);
ne ... rien (nothing), e.g. *Je ne veux rien* (I don't want anything).

Making questions

The simplest way to make a question is to give a sentence the intonation of a question – raise your voice at the end, e.g. *Il aime Anne* (He likes Anne) becomes *Il aime Anne?* (Does he like Anne?). This is everyday, spoken French.

Another way is to put *Est-ce que...?* at the beginning of the sentence, e.g. *Est-ce qu'il aime Anne?* (Does he like Anne?)

In more formal, polite French, you change the order of the words, e.g. *Voulez-vous du café?* (Would you like some coffee?) "T" goes between the verb and its subject if two vowels clash, e.g. *Aime-t-il Anne?* (Does he like Anne?).

As in English, many questions are formed using a special word like *pourquoi* (why?). The question is made in one of the three usual ways:
with no change to the sentence: *Pourquoi tu veux ça?* (Why do you want that?);
with *est-ce que*: *Pourquoi est-ce que tu veux ça?*;
with a change of order: *Pourquoi veux-tu ça?*

These words can be used in the same ways:

who?	*qui?*	where?	*où?*
what	*quoi?*	how much?	*combien?*
when?	*quand?*	which?	*quel?*
how?	*comment?*	what?	

Numbers, colours, countries etc.

Numbers

0	zéro	17	dix-sept	82	quatre-vingt-deux	
1	un	18	dix-huit	90	quatre-vingt-dix[1]	
2	deux	19	dix-neuf	91	quatre-vingt-onze[1]	
3	trois	20	vingt	92	quatre-vingt-douze[1]	
4	quatre	21	vingt et un	100	cent	
5	cinq	22	vingt-deux	101	cent un	
6	six	23	vingt-trois	200	deux cents	
7	sept	30	trente	300	trois cents	
8	huit	31	trente et un	1,000	mille	
9	neuf	40	quarante	1,100	onze cents[2]	
10	dix	50	cinquante	1,200	douze cents[2]	
11	onze	60	soixante	2,000	deux mille	
12	douze	70	soixante-dix[1]	2,100	deux mille cent	
13	treize	71	soixante et onze[1]	10,000	dix mille	
14	quatorze	72	soixante-douze[1]	100,000	cent mille	
15	quinze	80	quatre-vingts	1,000,000	un million	
16	seize	81	quatre-vingt-un			

Colours

colour	la couleur
light	clair/claire
dark	foncé/foncée
black	noir/noire
blue	bleu/bleue
navy	bleu marine
brown	marron, brun/ brune
green	vert/verte
grey	gris/grise
orange	orange
pink	rose
purple	mauve
red	rouge
white	blanc/blanche
yellow	jaune

Time

hour	l'heure
minute	la minute
morning	le matin
afternoon	l'après-midi
evening	le soir
midday	midi
midnight	minuit

What time is it?	Quelle heure est-il?
It's 1 o'clock.	Il est une heure.
2 o'clock	deux heures
a quarter past two	deux heures et quart
half past two	deux heures et demie
a quarter to two	deux heures moins le quart
five past two	deux heures cinq
ten to two	deux heures moins dix
What time...?	A quelle heure...?
in ten minutes	dans dix minutes
half an hour ago	il y a une demi-heure
at 09.00	à neuf heures
at 13.17	à treize heures dix-sept
at 9 a.m.	à neuf heures du matin
at 3 p.m.	à trois heures de l'après-midi
at 9 in the evening	à neuf heures du soir

1990	mille neuf cent quatre-vingt-dix
1991	mille neuf cent quatre-vingt-onze
1999	mille neuf cent quatre-vingt-dix-neuf

day	le jour
week	la semaine
month	le mois
year	l'année, l'an
diary	un journal
calendar	un calendrier
yesterday	hier
before yesterday	avant-hier
today	aujourd'hui
the next day	le lendemain
tomorrow	demain
after tomorrow	après-demain
last week	la semaine dernière
this week	cette semaine
next week	la semaine prochaine

Days and dates

Monday	lundi	March	mars
Tuesday	mardi	April	avril
Wednesday	mercredi	May	mai
Thursday	jeudi	June	juin
Friday	vendredi	July	juillet
Saturday	samedi	August	août
Sunday	dimanche	September	septembre
		October	octobre
January	janvier	November	novembre
February	février	December	décembre

What's the date?	Quelle est la date?
on Monday	le lundi
in August	en août
1st April	le premier avril
2nd January	le deux janvier

Seasons and weather

season	la saison	autumn	l'automne
spring	le printemps	winter	l'hiver
summer	l'été		

What's the weather like?	Quel temps fait-il?
weather forecast	la météo
It's fine.	Il fait beau.
It's sunny.	Il fait du soleil.
It's hot.	Il fait chaud.
It's horrible.	Il fait mauvais.
It's cold.	Il fait froid.
It's windy.	Il fait du vent.
It's raining.	Il pleut.
It's snowing.	Il neige.
It's foggy.	Il y a du brouillard.
It's freezing.	On gèle.
It's icy.	Il y a du verglas.
sky	le ciel
sun	le soleil
clouds	les nuages
rain	la pluie
waterproof	un imper, un imperméable
umbrella	le parapluie

[1]In Belgium and Switzerland, 70, 71, 72 etc. are septante, septante et un, septante-deux etc., and 90, 91 etc., are nonante, nonante et un etc. [2]For 1,000, 2,000 etc. you can also say mille cent, mille deux cents etc.

Countries and continents

world	*le monde*	Greece	*la Grèce*
continent	*le continent*	Hungary	*la Hongrie*
country	*le pays*	India	*l'Inde (f)*
border	*la frontière*	Ireland	*l'Irlande (f)*
north	*le nord*	Israel	*Israël (m)*
south	*le sud*	Italy	*l'Italie (f)*
east	*l'est*	Jamaica	*la Jamaïque*
west	*l'ouest*	Japan	*le Japon*
		Martinique	*la Martinique*
Africa	*l'Afrique (f)*	Middle East	*le Moyen-Orient*
Algeria	*l'Algérie (f)*	Morocco	*le Maroc*
Asia	*l'Asie (f)*	Netherlands	*les Pays-Bas*
Australia	*l'Australie (f)*	New Zealand	*la Nouvelle-*
Austria	*l'Autriche (f)*		*Zélande*
Bangladesh	*le Bangladesh*	North Africa	*l'Afrique du*
Belgium	*la Belgique*		*Nord*
Canada	*le Canada*	Pakistan	*le Pakistan*
Caribbean	*les Petites*	Poland	*la Pologne*
Islands	*Antilles (f)*	Scotland	*l'Ecosse (f)*
Central	*l'Amérique*	South America	*l'Amérique du*
America	*centrale (f)*		*Sud (f)*
China	*la Chine*	Spain	*l'Espagne (f)*
Corsica	*la Corse*	Switzerland	*la Suisse*
England	*l'Angleterre (f)*	Tunisia	*la Tunisie*
Europe	*l'Europe (f)*	Turkey	*la Turquie*
France	*la France*	United States	*les Etats-Unis*
Germany	*l'Allemagne (f)*	USSR	*l'URSS (f)*
Great Britain	*la Grande-*	Vietnam	*le Viêt-Nam*
	Bretagne	Wales	*le Pays de Galles*

Nationalities

You can either say *Je viens de/
d'/du/des*[3]... (I come from...) +
country, e.g. *Je viens d'Angleterre*
or *Je suis...* (I am...) + adjective
for nationality, e.g.:

American	*américain/américaine*
Australian	*australien/australienne*
Belgian	*belge*
Canadian	*canadien/canadienne*
English	*anglais/anglaise*
French	*français/française*
Irish	*irlandais/irlandaise*
Scottish	*écossais/écossaise*
Swiss	*suisse*

Faiths and beliefs

agnostic	*un agnostique*
atheist	*un/une athée*
Buddhist	*bouddhiste*
Catholic	*catholique*
Christian	*chrétien/chrétienne*
Hindu	*hindou/hindoue*
Jewish	*juif/juive*
Muslim	*musulman/*
	musulmane
Protestant	*protestant/*
	protestante
Sikh	*sikh*

Fact file

This Fact file supplies information on Belgium
and Switzerland. It focuses on the essential,
practical facts that differ from information
given for France.

Belgium

Languages – French is mostly spoken in the
south and Flemish in the north.
Travel – For anyone under 26, cheap deals
include the *TTB* (train, tram, bus) and the
Tourrail card, both valid on the *SNCB*
(Belgian national railways). Taxis take up to
four passengers but can be expensive.
Mopeds can be ridden from age 16.
Banks, post offices, phones – Currency is the
Belgian *franc* (BF). 1 BF = 100 *centimes*.
Banking hours are usually 9-12 and 2-4. In
big cities some banks stay open at lunchtime.
Phones are either coin or card operated.
Télécartes (phonecards) are widely available.
Shopping – Opening times are 9 to 6 or later
on Friday. Shops close on Sunday and on one
other day. Look out for signs on shop doors
saying which day they close. Chain stores
include *Noprix*, *GB* and *Delhaize*.
Emergencies – Dial 100 for police, fire and
ambulance. (From 1992 dial 112.)

Switzerland

Languages – The three official languages are
French, German and Italian.
Travel – Cheap rail deals include *Swiss Pass,
Swiss Card* and *Swiss Flexi Pass*. These also
entitle you to reductions on most bus and lake
steamer services. The *PTT* (post office) runs
bus services to remote areas; multiple-journey
tickets work out cheaper. Some cities have a
system of cheap day tickets for local transport.
You can hire bikes from train stations but you
must book the day before. You have to be 18
to ride a moped. On motorways buy a
vignette (tax sticker) at the border.
Banks, post offices, phones – The currency is
the Swiss *franc* (SF). 1 SF = 100 *centimes*.
Banking hours vary. In cities banks open 8.30-
4.30 on weekdays, elsewhere they close for
lunch from 12-2. Chain stores, e.g. *Migros*
and *Co-op*, often change money. Phone
boxes mainly take coins.
Shopping – Opening times vary a lot. Shops
tend to open earlier than in France, and some
are closed on Monday mornings.
Emergencies – There is no national health service
so make sure you are insured. Phone numbers:
police, 117; fire, 118; ambulance, 144.

[3]*Je viens de* + (f) name, *d'* + names that start with a vowel, *du* + (m) names, *des* + plural
names. See page 51.

Index

This Index lists the most essential words. If you can't find the word you want, look up a relevant entry, e.g. to find "garlic" look under "vegetables". Adjectives with two forms are given twice: (m) followed by (f) (see page 51), and verbs are in the infinitive (see page 52).

bus, 6, 7	le bus, l'autobus (m)
bus station, 7	la gare routière
bus stop, 7	l'arrêt d'autobus (m)
busy, 30	pris/prise
butter, 20	le beurre
to buy, 6	acheter
bye, 3	salut
cable TV, 33	la télé câblée
café, 16-17	le café, le bar
cake, 25	le gâteau
(telephone) call, 13	la communication
to call, 13, 15	appeler
to call back, 15	rappeler
calm, 8	calme
to camp, 10	camper
camping, campsite 10-11	le camping
to cancel, 8	annuler
can opener, 11	l'ouvre-boîte (m)
car, 9	la voiture, la bagnole*
parts of, 9	
caravan, 11	la caravane
career, 45	la carrière
car park, 5	le parking
carrier bag, 25	le sac plastique
to carry	porter
to carry on, 4	continuer
cashier's desk, 15	la caisse
cassette, 28	la cassette
castle, 30	le château
casualty department, 47	le service des urgences
to catch, 39	attraper
cathedral, 30	la cathédrale
to cause trouble, 47	faire des ennuis
cave, 30	la grotte
chair, 16	la chaise
to change, 6, 8	changer
changing room, 27	la cabine d'essayage
channel (TV), 33	la chaîne
charter flight, 8	le vol charter
charts (music), 29	le hit-parade
cheap, 11	pas cher/chère
to cheat, 39	tricher
to check in, 8	enregistrer
check-out, 22	la caisse
cheers, 16	à ta/votre santé
cheese, 16, 18	le fromage
chemist, 22, 46	la pharmacie
chicken, 21	le poulet
chips, 18	les frites (f pl)
chocolate, 25	le chocolat
church, 5, 30	l'église (f)
cigarette	la cigarette
cinema, 5, 30, 33	le cinéma
clean, 11	propre
clever, 36	doué/douée
close, 5	près (de)
closed, 22	fermé/fermée
clothes, 26-27	les vêtements (m pl)
club, 30	la boîte (de nuit)
club (sports), 39	le club
coach (bus), 7	le car
coast, 30	la côte
(telephone) code, 14	l'indicatif (m)
coffee, 16, 21	le café
black	le café, l'express (m)
white	le crème, le café au lait
coke, 16	le coca
cold, 11, 13	froid/froide
a cold, 46	un rhume
to collect, 44	faire collection de
college, 42	le lycée
types of, 43	
colour, 24, 26, 54	la couleur
to come, 37, 53	venir
a comic, 33	une BD, une bande dessinée
commercial, 33	commercial/ commerciale
compact disc, 28	le disque compact
completely, 36	complètement
computer, 44	l'ordinateur (m)
concert, 29	le concert
to confirm, 8	confirmer
constipated, 46	constipé/constipée
contact lens, 47	le verre de contact
cool, 27, 37	branché/branchée*, cool*
corner, 5	le coin
to cost, 9	coûter
countries, 55	
countryside, 30	la campagne
cramp, 46	la crampe
crash helmet, 9	le casque
crazy, 37, 49	fou/folle, dingue*
credit card, 15	la carte de crédit
a creep, 37	un pauvre type
crisps, 25	les chips (f pl)
to cross, 4	traverser
crossroads, 4	le carrefour
curly, 36	frisé/frisée
currency, 15	
currents, 40	les courants (m pl)
customs, 8	la douane
to cut, 46	couper
cut price, 8	à prix réduit
to dance, 30, 36	danser
danger, 47	le danger
dangerous, 40	dangereux/ dangereuse
dark (colouring), 36	brun/brune
dates, 54	
day, 54	le jour
day after tomorrow, day, 30, 54	après-demain
dead end, 5	le cul-de-sac
delay, 8	le retard
delicious, 21	délicieux/délicieuse
demo, 45	la manifestation

dentist, 46	le dentiste
deodorant, 12	le déodorant
department store, 22	le grand magasin
departure gate, 8	la porte (de départ)
departures, 7	les départs (m pl)
depressed, 37	déprimé/déprimée
dessert, 18	le dessert
diarrhoea, 46	la diarrhée
dictionary, 46	le dictionnaire
difficult, 44	difficile
dinner, 11, 21	le dîner
(film) director, 33	le réalisateur/la réalisatrice
(telephone) directory, 15	l'annuaire (m)
discipline, 43	la discipline
disco, 30	la boîte, la discothèque
divorced, 35	divorcé/divorcée
dizzy, 46	la tête qui tourne
to do, 34	faire
to do (study), 42, 43	étudier
doctor, 46	le docteur, le médecin, la femme docteur
(car) documents, 9	les papiers (m pl)
doubles, 39	le double
doughnut, 25	le beignet
downstairs, 13	en bas
a draw (sports), 39	un match nul
to draw, 4	dessiner
(salad) dressing, 18	la vinaigrette
dressy, 27	habillé/habillée
drink, 17	la boisson
types of, 16-17	
to drink, 11, 16	boire
to go for a drink, 30	aller prendre un pot
drinking water, 11, 47	l'eau potable (f)
not drinking water, 47	eau non potable
to drive	conduire
driving licence, 9	le permis de conduire
drugs, 45	les drogues (f pl)
to dry, 12	sécher
dubbed, 33	doublé/doublée
dull, boring, 30	ennuyeux/ennuyeuse
easy, 44	facile
easy going, 43	pas strict/stricte, sympa
to eat, 16	manger
eating, 16-17, 18-19, 20-21	
egg, 21	l'oeuf (m)
electric socket, 13	la prise
emergencies, 47	
emergency exit, 47	la sortie de secours
end of, at the end of, 5	au bout de
engine, 9	le moteur
English, 3	l'anglais (m)
enough, 21, 25, 41	assez
enquiries, 15	le bureau de renseignements
entertainment guide, 30	le programme des spectacles
entrance, 22	l'entrée (f)
environment, 45	l'environnement (m)
evening, 13, 30, 54	le soir
every day, 7	tous les jours
exams, 43	les examens (m pl)
except, 7	sauf
exchange (holiday), 35	l'échange (m)
exchange rate, 15	le cours du change
exciting, 33	passionnant/ passionnante
excuse me, 3, 19	pardon, s'il vous plaît
exhibition, 30	l'exposition (f)
exit, 22	la sortie
to expect, 15	attendre
expelled, 43	renvoyé/renvoyée
expensive, 11, 41	cher/chère
to explain, 45	expliquer
extra, 13	un/une autre
eye, 36	l'oeil (m) (pl les yeux)
fair (colouring), 36	blond/blonde
family, 35	la famille
fan (music), 29	le fan
far, 5	loin
fare, 7	le tarif
fashion, 27	la mode
fashionable, 27	à la mode
fat, 36	gros/grosse
father, 35	le père
to be fed up, 48	en avoir marre*
feminist, 45	féministe
ferry, 8	le ferry
film (camera), 24	la pellicule
film (cinema), 31, 32-33	le film
film buff, 33	le mordu/la mordue du cinéma
film showing, 30	la séance
to finish, 30, 42	finir
Fire!, 47	Au feu!
fire brigade, 47	les pompiers (m pl)
fireworks, 30	le feu d'artifice
first, 4	le premier/la première
fish, 18	le poisson
to fix, 9	réparer
flat (apartment), 35	l'appartement (m)
flea market, 22	le marché aux puces
flight, 8	le vol
flight number, 8	le numéro de vol
on the floor, 13	par terre
flu, 46	la grippe
to follow, 4, 47	suivre
food, 16, 18-19, 21, 23, 25	la cuisine
food poisoning, 46	l'empoisonnement alimentaire (m)
foot passenger, 8	le passager sans véhicule
foreign exchange, foreign exchange office, 15	le bureau de change
fork, 21	la fourchette
fountain, 31	la fontaine

free (empty), 16 — libre
free (school), 43 — gratuit/gratuite
French, 3 — le français
friend, 36 — l'ami/l'amie
fruit, 18, 25 — les fruits (m pl)
fruit juice, 16 — le jus de fruit
fruit/veg stall, 22 — le marchand de fruits et légumes
full, 10 — complet
fun, 33 — marrant/marrante
funny, 33 — drôle
the future, 45 — l'avenir (m)

a game of, 38, 39 — une partie de
games, 44 — les jeux (m pl)
garage, 9 — le garage
garlic, 21 — l'ail (m)
gay, 45 — gay, homo
gears, 9 — les vitesses (f pl)
(hair) gel, 24 — le gel (pour les cheveux)
gig, 29 — le concert
girl, 36 — la fille
girlfriend, 35 — la petite amie
glass, 16 — le verre
glasses, 47 — les lunettes (f pl)
to go, 4, 53 — aller
to go out with, 37 — sortir avec
goal, 39 — le but
god, 45 — dieu
goggles, 40 — les lunettes de plongée (f pl)
good, 33, 43 — bon/bonne
goodbye, 3, 13 — au revoir
good-looking, 36 — beau/belle
not good-looking, 36 — pas beau/pas belle
in a good mood, 37 — de bonne humeur
gossip, 36-37
grant (student), 43 — la bourse
greengrocer, 22 — le marchand de fruits et légumes
greetings, 3, 12
group (musicians), 29 — le groupe, l'orchestre (m)
guide book, 30 — le guide
guy, 36 — le type

hair, 36 — les cheveux (m pl)
hairdryer, 12 — le sèche-cheveux
ham, 16 — le jambon
hamburger, 18 — le hamburger
handbag, 47 — le sac à main
hand luggage, 8 — les bagages à main (m pl)
hang on, 15 — ne quittez pas
hangover, 46 — la gueule de bois
happy, 37 — heureux/heureuse
to have, 3, 52 — avoir
hayfever, 46 — le rhume des foins
(to have a) headache, 46 — (avoir) mal à la tête
headphones, 28 — le casque
health food shop, 22 — le magasin de produits diététiques

to hear, 29 — écouter
heavy, 8 — lourd/lourde
hello, 3, 12 — bonjour
Help!, 47 — Au secours!
to help, 4, 20 — aider
here, 5, 34 — ici
Hi!, 3 — Salut!
hi-fi, 28 — la chaîne hi-fi
to hire, 9 — louer
  bikes and mopeds, 9
  skis, 41
hit (music), 29 — le tube
to hitch, 9 — faire du stop
holiday, 35, 43 — les vacances (f pl)
homework, 43 — les devoirs (m pl)
horrible, 36 — pas sympa, mauvais/ mauvaise, vache*
hospital, 47 — l'hôpital (m)
hot, 11 — chaud/chaude
(too) hot, spicy, 21 — (trop) relevé/relevée
hot chocolate, 16 — le chocolat chaud
hotel, 10 — l'hôtel (m)
house, 35 — la maison
hovercraft, 8 — l'aéroglisseur (m)
How?, 3 — Comment?
How are you?, 12 — Comment allez-vous?
How long? (time), 34 — Combien de temps?
How many?, 3 — Combien?
How much?, 3 — Combien?
How much is it?, 3, 22 — C'est combien?, Ça coûte combien?
How often?, 38 — Tous les combien?
(to be) hungry, 3 — (avoir) faim
to hurt a little, 46 — faire un peu mal
to hurt a lot, 46 — faire très mal
husband, 35 — le mari

with ice, 16 — avec des glaçons (m pl)
ice-cream, 16 — la glace
ID, 47 — les papiers (m pl)
idea, 30 — l'idée (f)
an idiot, 37 — un crétin/une crétine
I'd like..., 3 — Je voudrais...
important, 45 — important/importante
ill — malade
illness, 46-47
I'm lost., 47 — Je suis perdu/perdue.
in, 5 — dans
indoor, 39 — couvert/couverte
infection, 46 — l'infection (f)
information, 8 — les renseignements (m pl)
in front of, 5 — devant
injection, 46 — la piqûre
(musical) instrument, 29 — l'instrument (m)
insurance, 9, 47 — l'assurance (f)
interesting, 30 — intéressant/ intéressante
interests, 44
Is there...?, 3 — Est-ce qu'il y a...?
It/this is..., 3 — C'est...

jacket, 27	la veste
jam, 21	la confiture
jealous, 37	jaloux/jalouse
jeans, 26	le jean
job, 45	le boulot
journey, 6	le voyage
junction, 4	le carrefour
Keep out, 47	Défense d'entrer
ketchup, 18	le ketchup
key, 11, 13, 47	la clé
kind (type), 28	le genre
to kiss, 37	embrasser
knife, 21	le couteau
to know, 3, 36	savoir, connaître
laid-back, 37	relax/relaxe*
lake, 30	le lac
languages, 42	les langues (f pl)
large, 16	grand/grande
last, 7	le dernier
later, 45	plus tard
latest, 7	dernier/dernière
launderette, 22	la laverie automatique
to lay the table, 20	mettre la table
lazy, 37	paresseux/paresseuse
to learn, 29	apprendre
to leave, 15	laisser
to leave (depart), 7	partir
lecture, 43	le cours
lecturer, 43	le prof, le maître de conférences
left, 4	à gauche
left luggage locker, 7	le casier de consigne
lemon, 16	le citron
a slice of, 16	une tranche de
less, 25	moins
lesson (school), 43	le cours
lesson (sports), 41	la leçon
letter, 15	la lettre
library, 33	la bibliothèque
lifeguard, 47	le maître-nageur
to like	aimer
to listen, 28	écouter
litre, 9	le litre
a little, 20	un petit peu, un peu
live (music), 29	en direct
to live, 34, 35	habiter
to live with, 35	habiter chez
liver, 21	le foie
loads, 42	plein
long, 27, 36	long/longue
loo, 12	les toilettes, les cabinets, les WC
loo paper, 11	le papier hygiénique
look (style), 27	le look
to look, 24	regarder
to look for, 10	chercher
to lose, 14, 39	perdre
lost, 4	perdu/perdue
lost property, 47	objets perdus (m pl)
loud, 28	fort/forte
lousy, 33	mauvais/mauvaise
to love, 40	adorer
luggage, 8	les bagages (m pl)
lunch, 11	le déjeuner
machine, 6	la machine
macho, 37	macho
mad, 37, 49	fou/folle, dingue*
Madam, Mrs, 3, 12	Madame
main, 4	principal/principale
main course, 18	le plat principal
make-up, 24	du maquillage (m)
man	l'homme (m)
map, 4, 5	le plan, la carte
march, demo, 45	la manifestation, la manif
margarine, 21	la margarine
market, 22	le marché
married, 35	marié/mariée
mask, 40	le masque
match (sports), 39	le match
matches, 11	les allumettes (f pl)
mate, 36	le copain/la copine
maybe, 3	peut-être
mayonnaise, 18	la mayonnaise
meal, 21	le repas
to mean, 3	vouloir dire
meat, 18, 21	la viande
medicine, 46	le médicament
medium, 27	moyen/moyenne
to meet, 8, 31	rencontrer, se retrouver
menu, 16, 19	la carte, le menu
message, 15	le message
milk, 16	le lait
milkshake, 16	le milk-shake
mineral water, 16	l'eau minérale (f)
fizzy	gazeuse
still	plate
Miss, 3	Mademoiselle
mixed up, 37	compliqué/ compliquée
money, 14, 15, 47	l'argent (m)
month, 54	le mois
mood, 37	l'humeur (f)
moped, 9	un vélomoteur
more, 25	plus
morning, 30, 54	le matin
mosquito, 46	le moustique
mother, 35	la mère
motorbike, 9	la moto
motorway, 5	l'autoroute (f)
mountain, 30	la montagne
movie, 33	le film
Mr, Sir, 3, 12	Monsieur
Mrs, Madam, 3, 12	Madame
museum, 5, 30	le musée
music, 28-29	la musique
music/pop video, 28	le clip
mustard, 18	la moutarde
name, 35	le nom
nasty, 36	mauvais/mauvaise, vache*
nationalities, 55	
national service, 43	le service militaire

near, 5 — *près (de)*
nearby, 5 — *tout près, juste à côté*
new, 29 — *nouveau/nouvelle*
news, 33 — *les informations (f pl)*
newspaper, 24 — *le journal (pl les journaux)*
next, 6, 7 — *le prochain/la prochaine*
next to, 5 — *près de*
nice, 13 — *gentil/gentille*
nice (OK), 36 — *sympa*
nickname, 35 — *le surnom*
night, 11 — *la nuit*
nightclub, 30 — *la boîte (de nuit)*
no, 3 — *non*
nobody, 53 — *personne*
no entry, 5, 47 — *sens interdit, défense d'entrer*
no parking, 5 — *stationnement interdit*
no smoking, 8 — *non-fumeurs*
no swimming, 47 — *baignade interdite*
note (money), 15 — *le billet*
novel, 33 — *le roman*
now, nowadays, 45 — *de nos jours, maintenant*
nuclear disarmament, 45 — *le désarmement nucléaire*
nuclear power, 45 — *l'énergie nucléaire (f)*
number, 15 — *le numéro*
number one (record), 29 — *le numéro un*
numbers, 3, 54

offbeat, 33 — *original/originale*
oil, 9 — *l'huile (f)*
OK, 36 — *bien*
OK (looks), 36 — *pas mal*
OK (nice), 36 — *sympa*
old — *vieux/vieille*
old-fashioned, 36 — *ringard/ringarde**
omelette, 16 — *l'omelette (f)*
on, 5 — *sur*
one way, 5 — *sens unique*
open, 22 — *ouvert/ouverte*
opposite, 5 — *en face de*
optician, 46 — *l'opticien (m)*
or, 3 — *ou*
orange juice, 16 — *le jus d'orange*
to order, 18 — *demander*
other — *autre*
(some) other time, 37 — *une autre fois*
outdoor, 39 — *en plein air*
out-of-date, 27 — *démodé/démodée*
over, 5 — *par-dessus*
over the top, 33 — *exagéré/exagérée*

pal, 36 — *le copain/la copine*
papers (personal), 47 — *les papiers (m pl)*
parcel, 15 — *le colis*
parents, 35 — *les parents (m pl)*
park, 5 — *le jardin public*
parking meter, 5 — *le parcmètre*
part-time job, 44 — *le petit boulot*
party, 30 — *la fête, la boum*

to pass, 20 — *passer*
passport, 8, 47 — *le passeport*
(in) the past, 45 — *(dans) le passé*
pasta, 21 — *les pâtes (f pl)*
path, footpath, 4 — *le chemin, le sentier*
pavement, 5 — *le trottoir*
to pay, 11, 13 — *payer*
peace, 45 — *la paix*
peanuts, 25 — *les cacahuètes (f pl)*
pedestrian crossing, 4 — *le passage clouté*
pedestrians, 5 — *les piétons (m pl)*
pen, ballpoint, 24 — *le stylo*
people, 10 — *les personnes (f pl)*
pepper, 18 — *le poivre*
performance (film), 30 — *la séance*
period, 46 — *les règles (f pl)*
personal stereo, 28 — *le baladeur*
petrol, 9 — *l'essence (f)*
petrol station, 9 — *la station-service*
phone, 13, 14-15 — *le téléphone*
phone box, 13 — *la cabine téléphonique*
phonecard, 15 — *la télécarte*
phone number, 15 — *le numéro de téléphone*
photography, 33, 44 — *la photographie*
picnic, 30 — *le pique-nique*
pill, 46 — *le cachet, la pilule*
pizza, 18 — *la pizza*
plants, 45 — *les plantes (f pl)*
plate, 21 — *l'assiette (f)*
platform, 7 — *le quai*
play (theatre), 33 — *la pièce*
to play, 29, 38 — *jouer*
please, 3 — *s'il vous plaît, s'il te plaît*
pocket money, 44 — *l'argent de poche (m)*
poetry, 33 — *la poésie*
police, 47 — *la police*
police station, 47 — *le commissariat de police*
political, 33 — *politique*
politics, 45 — *la politique*
pollution, 45 — *la pollution*
poor, 45 — *pauvre*
pork, 21 — *le porc*
port, 8 — *le port*
postbox, 15 — *la boîte aux lettres*
postcard, 15, 24 — *la carte postale*
poste restante, 15 — *la poste restante*
post office, 5 — *la poste, les PTT (f pl)*
power (electricity), 47 — *le courant*
to prefer, 40 — *préférer*
pregnant — *enceinte*
pretty, 36 — *joli/jolie*
price, 18, 22 — *le prix*
private property, 47 — *la propriété privée*
problems, 47 — *les ennuis (m pl)*
programme (TV), 33 — *le programme*
to have a puncture, 9 — *crever*
to put, 12 — *mettre*

qualifications, 45 — *les diplômes (m pl)*
Quick!, 39 — *Vite!*

spaghetti, 18	les spaghettis (m pl)
spare time, 44	le temps libre
to speak, 3	parler
to split, 26	déchirer
to split up (a couple), 37	casser
spoon, 21	la cuillère
sport, 38-39, 40-41	le sport
sports centre, 39	le centre sportif
square, 4	la place, le square
square (old-fashioned), 36	ringard/ringarde*
stadium, 39	le stade
stairs, 22	l'escalier (m)
stamp, 15	le timbre
standby, 8	sans garantie
to start, 30	commencer
starter, 18	l'entrée (f)
(radio) station, 28	la station
(railway) station, 7	la gare
to stay, 35	rester
steak, 18	le steak
medium	à point
rare	saignant
well done	bien cuit
to steal, 47	voler
(to have a) stomach ache, 46	(avoir) mal au ventre
straight (hair), 36	raide
straight ahead, 4	tout droit
street, 4	la rue, le boulevard
strict, 43	strict/stricte, sévère
strong, 40	fort/forte
stuck up, 37	snob
student, 42	l'étudiant/l'étudiante
student fare, 7	le tarif étudiant
student ticket, 30	le billet étudiant
to study, 35	étudier
(to be) stung, 46	(être) piqué/piquée
style, 27	le style
subject, 42, 43	la matière
with subtitles, 33	sous-titré/titrée
suburbs, 5	la banlieue
subway, 4	le passage souterrain
sugar, 16	le sucre
suitcase, 8	la valise
sun, 40	le soleil
to sunbathe, 40	se faire bronzer
sunglasses, 23	les lunettes de soleil (f pl)
sunscreen, 24	l'écran total (m)
sunstroke, 46	le coup de soleil
sun-tan lotion, 24	la crème solaire
supermarket, 22	le supermarché, le libre-service, le magasin d'alimentation générale
to support (a team), 45	être pour
surfboard, 40	la planche de surf
surname, 35	le nom de famille
sweet (taste), 21	sucré/sucrée
sweets, 25	les bonbons (m pl)
to swim, 11, 40	se baigner, nager
swimming pool, 11	la piscine
swimsuit/trunks, 27	le maillot (de bain)
table, 16	la table
to take, 4	prendre
take-away, 18	à emporter
tall, 36	grand/grande
tape, 28	la cassette
to tape, 28	enregistrer
tap water, 11	l'eau du robinet (f)
taxi, 8	le taxi
tea, 16	le thé
teacher, 43	le professeur, le/la prof
team, 39	l'équipe (f)
telephone, 13, 14-15	le téléphone
telephone box, 15	la cabine téléphonique
to tell, 15	dire
telly, TV, 33	la télé
temperature, 46	la température
tent, 11	la tente
term, 43	le trimestre
beginning of term, 43	la rentrée
thank you, 3	merci
theatre, 33	le théâtre
there, 5	là
there is/are, 3	il y a
thick, 37	bête
thin, 36	mince
things, 12, 47	les affaires (f pl), les trucs* (m pl)
to think, 32, 45	penser
to think about, 24	réfléchir
third, 4	troisième
Third World, 45	le Tiers-Monde
(to be) thirsty, 21	(avoir) soif
to throw, 39	lancer
ticket, 6, 7, 8, 30	le ticket, le billet
ticket machine, 7	le distributeur automatique
ticket office, 7, 30	le guichet
tight, 27	serré/serrée
till, 15	la caisse
time	le temps
time (telling the), 6, 54	l'heure (f)
timetable, 7	l'horaire (m)
tired, 13	fatigué/fatiguée
tissue, 24	le mouchoir en papier
today, 30, 54	aujourd'hui
toilet, 12	les toilettes (f pl), les cabinets (m pl)
toilet paper, 11	le papier hygiénique
toilet, public, 4	les toilettes publiques (f pl)
gents (sign)	messieurs
ladies (sign)	dames
toll, 9	le péage
tomorrow, 30, 54	demain
tonight, 30, 54	ce soir
too, 21, 37	trop, aussi
(to have a) toothache, 46	(avoir) mal aux dents
toothpaste, 12	le dentifrice
the Top 50, 29	le Top 50 (cinquante)
tour (music), 29	la tournée

First published in 1990 by Usborne Publishing Ltd. Usborne House, 83-85 Saffron Hill London EC1N 8RT, England Copyright © 1990 Usborne Publishing Ltd.